STYLE COUNSEL

CREATING YOUR BEST LOOK

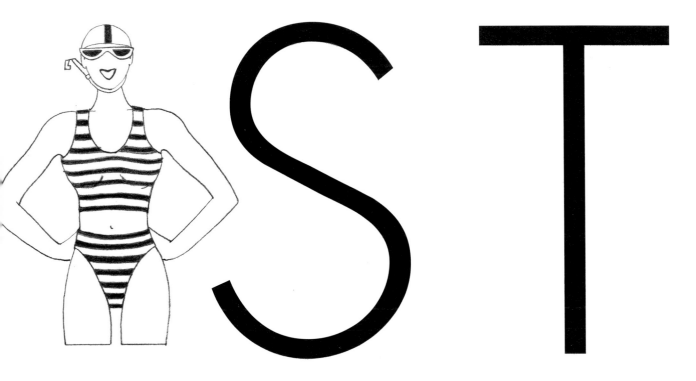

S T

CAROL SPENSER'S

YLE

COUNSEL

B🟫XTREE

First published in Great Britain in 1995 by
Boxtree Limited, Broadwall House, 21 Broadwall, London SE1 9PL

© Carol Spenser 1995

The right of Carol Spenser to be identified as Author of this work has
been asserted by her in accordance with the Copyright, Designs and
Patents Act 1988

ISBN 0 7522 0530 7

1 3 5 7 9 10 8 6 4 2

Designed by Hammond Hammond
Typeset by SX Composing, Rayleigh, Essex
Origination by Pica Colour Separations, Singapore
Printed and bound in Great Britain by Bath Press

A CIP catalogue entry for this book is available from the British Library

I WOULD LIKE TO DEDICATE THIS BOOK TO MY HUSBAND, DAVID, FOR HIS LOVE, SUPPORT AND BELIEF IN ME — BUT, MOST OF ALL, FOR HIS MONEY.

ACKNOWLEDGEMENTS

EXTRA SPECIAL THANKS to three people of very differing talents:

- *Doris Pooser* in New York — for being a great friend and colleague and an inspiration to would-be stylish women everywhere.
- *Margaret Bateman* in the barn in my garden — for dedication above and beyond the call of duty, including typing the original manuscript for this book from my scrawl.
- *Gary Hooker* at Saks, Newcastle — hairdresser extraordinaire, for most of the stunning styles in this book (and his mum for modelling on page 103).

HEARTFELT THANKS to the following illustrators who managed to produce in reality the pictures from inside my head.

- *Cath Knox* — for all the wonderful illustrations (and for managing not to make curvy mouths look like cats' bottoms . . .)
- *Anna-Louise Ridley* — for the witty cartoons in chapter 8 (any resemblance to persons living or dead is sheer coincidence).
- *Penny Sobr* — who has illustrated my features in *Woman's Journal* many times and penned the stylish lady for the front flap.
- *Roger Hammond* — for pulling the whole book together brilliantly and remaining calm while all around panicked at approaching deadlines.

GROVELLING THANKS to all my friends and colleagues in the world of fashion, hair and beauty and publishing for letting me beg, steal and borrow their pictures and merchandise:

- *Woman's Journal* — for loaning me several Fashion Counsel members for makeovers on pages 142, 146, 150, 154 (and for helping me get my career off the ground three years ago with my regular Fashion Counsel column).
- *Grattan* — for all the inside fashion pictures (and for a contract which gives me an excuse to go 'up North').
- *Dickens & Jones, Regent Street, London* — for all the fashions on the front cover (except the Doc Martens).
- *Boots Opticians* — for all the photography featuring glasses (including Mary's new specs on page 155).
- *L'Oreal Coiffure* — for hair photographs (and for loaning Gary Hooker to me on a regular basis).
- *Monet/Marvella/Triffari* — for the jewellery pictures (and constant supply of their pieces for makeovers).
- *Clarins* — for make-up pictures and use of their cosmetics for shade charts.
- *WeightWatchers* — for loaning the makeover pictures of Erica and Sam on pages 139 and 157.
- *SHE* magazine — for loaning makeover pictures of Helen, Julie and Pamela on pages 153, 149 and 145.
- *PRIMA* magazine — for loaning makeover pictures of Sarla on page 141.
- *Rex Features* — for archive pictures of Princess Diana and Elizabeth Taylor on pages 38 and 39.
- *Berlei* — lingerie picture on page 47.
- Herbert Johnson — hat picture on page 67.
- *Direct Dialogue* — for use of the market research quotes on which my business and this book have been founded.

SPECIAL AWARDS FOR PATIENCE AND ENDURANCE goes jointly to my agent, Mike Hollingsworth, and Boxtree's Michael Alcock, for waiting over two years for me to sit still long enough to write this book. I got there in the end.

CONTENTS

INTRODUCTION

W HEN I FIRST trained as a style consultant nearly ten years ago it was for two reasons: firstly, I wanted a part-time job after just having had my first child; secondly, and probably more importantly, I was thirty years old and wanted to find out what *really* suited me after a couple of decades of experimenting with different fashions, colours, cosmetics and hair-styles.

Some of the 'looks' in the past had worked well, while others were a complete disaster. The long, straight hair with centre parting

In search of style

Getting it right – angular hairstyle, earrrings and neckline with a fitted jacket and padded shoulders

worked well for me in the early Seventies in my student days with cropped tops and hipster trousers. But in the late Seventies when I began working in PR, with my soft hairstyle and Laura Ashley, puffed-sleeved dresses or pie-crust collars, I was a walking nightmare! The power suits of the early Eighties were quite a godsend as I seemed to suit the padded shoulders, nipped-in waists and shorter skirts – and, for the first time, I took the plunge and had my hair cut into a short and sharp 'bob', to rave reviews.

If you look back through your photo albums you will probably feel the same – that on some days or in some periods of your life you looked good and would like to have those photos around to show your grandchildren. Others you would just like to burn – if you haven't already done so! For many women the knack of 'looking good' seems, depressingly, to be a very 'hit and miss' affair, which, as you get older, seems unfortunately to be more 'miss' than 'hit'.

Training as a style consultant opened my eyes to the many reasons behind my sartorial successes and failures. The pieces of the jigsaw began to fall into place giving me a total picture of my future style guidelines.

The long, straight hair of university days and the geometric Eighties power cut suited me because of the angles in my face; the soft, curly styles did nothing to play up those angles. Puff sleeves didn't suit me because I have narrow, sloping shoulders – making it obvious why padded shoulders do. Pie-crust collars, or any high necklines, are a disaster because I have a short neck – I never knew this! Wide belts are a no-no because I'm short-waisted; gathered waistlines only emphasise my ample hips; and long skirts make me look as if a great weight has squashed me into the ground because I'm petite – just nudging 5'3".

You may or may not have noticed that so far I have not mentioned anything about colour – with which image or style consultants are mostly associated. To be honest, this is because I was not greatly enamoured of the colour analysis I was given on my training. I was made a 'Summer' (although great battles raged among other consultants as to whether I was really a 'Spring'). Frankly, I didn't like either of those colour palettes: 'Summer', made up of mostly sweet-pea pastels made me feel like a piece of my grandmother's wallpaper; while 'Spring', with its oranges and lime greens, had overtones of a fruity Carmen Miranda.

The fact is that none of these shades suited my personal taste in colour or my personality. At the time, I had a wardrobe of quite earthy colours and I remember that I went for my interview with the style company in a brown dress, with a wooden necklace. My favourite colours, to which I am always instinctively drawn, are nearly all neutrals – black, brown, grey, beige, etc. My current wardrobe looks like a sea of porridge punctuated with the odd chocolate-chip cookie and stick of licorice.

My children always laugh when I open my suitcase on holiday to reveal layer upon layer of beige outfits! But those are the colours I like. That's me. That's my 'personal style'.

Unfortunately, when I trained in the late 1980s, no one out

Post-baby style doldrums – horizontal lines, gathered waistlines, patch pockets, wide mid-calf skirt and flat shoes – all disastrous for my petite, pear-shaped figure.

there, consultants or customers, seemed interested in the style side of our business – customers wanted to have their colours done, and consultants seemed happy to perform hours of 'draping' and simply sell a swatch of colours and a set of make-up at the end of it. I did this for several years and even became a trainer myself (dressed as a sweet-pea) until frustration got the better of me and I decided to go it alone and spread my 'Style is Everything' message.

After I launched Public Persona in 1992 I discovered that in fact I was not alone out there, and there was little or no converting to do! I conducted an extensive market research survey with women of all ages, backgrounds and lifestyles and found that, with all the emphasis on colour analysis, we had only been reaching the tip of the iceberg with regard to the number of women who wanted advice about their appearance.

The hundreds of women I spoke to then, and the thousands who have since written to me via my regular magazine columns and TV appearances, all say the same things. They don't want to have to go home and throw out all their clothes just because an analyst has told them they're the 'wrong' colours. Many, like me, know which colours they like and want to stick to them; others want the freedom to follow the changing colours of the fashion world. Not many want to be put into restrictive colour 'seasons' or other rigid boxes governed by a swatch wallet.

What women *do* tell me they want advice about are hairstyles, cosmetic techniques, choosing accessories and, most importantly of all, how to understand the good and not-so-good aspects of their bodies to help them make better fashion decisions and minimise all those dreadful fashion mistakes at the back of the wardrobe. Style advice rather than colour rules.

By the end of the last chapter, you will have the blueprint for your future personal style that you will be able to adapt to the ever-changing fashion styles and colours, if you so wish.

Getting it wrong again – a too-wispy hairstyle and a superb example of how disastrous a straight dress can look on a curvy figure – even though taupe was one of my recommended 'Summer' colours.

IN SEARCH OF STYLE

CHAPTER ONE

WHY YOUR FACE IS THE BEST STARTING POINT

WHEN I START a makeover, whether for a magazine, on TV or in a private consultation, I always start at the top – with the face and all that frames it. This includes hair, necklines, jewellery, plus glasses and hats if the person wears them. Your face,

'I think my face is round ... but then again it could be square.'

Susan, age 25

like it or not, is the focal point of the body. When someone meets you, they look at your face first and then, without realising it, their eye travels rapidly down and up

your body until it settles on your face again where eye contact is usually maintained.

Knowing that your face, hair, glasses, etc are looking their best gives you enormous confidence. Even if you are not overjoyed about your figure, are pregnant or even trying to lose weight, feeling good about the most unique part of yourself gives a real boost. And your face *is* your most unique asset; bodies can look amazingly similar, but faces (excepting identical twins of course!) are as individual as fingerprints.

What you choose to do with and around your face is also one of the best ways of expressing your personality – particularly if you have a job which requires you to wear a uniform daily. Two women at a wedding could wear the same plain classic suit, but their wildly different choices of hairstyle, hat and jewellery could indicate that their personalities are as different as chalk and cheese.

The face has been called 'the window to the soul' and I would agree with that because it says so much about who you are. As your

face

life changes and your personality develops in different ways, you need, however, to keep reassessing that message. Hanging on to the same hairstyle, make-up and jewellery from your twenties is rarely appropriate or flattering to a woman now in her forties or fifties. A soft, curly hairstyle and round earrings may have suited you as a curvaceous twenty-something but, if age has given you a more angular face, a short, slick hairstyle with straighter earrings will look stunning – and take years off your age!

Keep reassessing your hairstyle, jewellery and necklines to make sure they suit your face shape and features.

DEFINING YOUR FACE OUTLINE

The best *shape* of hairstyle is determined by the outline of your face. I have found that most people haven't a clue about their face outline, and very often think it is the complete opposite of what it really is! (This is why I always ask for a close-up head and shoulders photo when compiling a Personal Profile.)

The most accurate way to assess your face outline is to pin back all the hair from your face and look directly into a mirror. (Do this in the bathroom, with plenty of make-up remover and tissues handy, as it can be rather messy!) Keep one eye closed and with the opposite hand draw around the reflection of the outline of your face, starting at the hairline, with an old lipstick, eye-pencil or mascara. Compare the outline with the list below for the closest match – then clean the mirror quickly before it dries!

CURVED OUTLINES

Oval. The forehead may be slightly wider than the rest of the face and the sides taper gently inwards towards the jaw. The oval is often called the 'perfect' face shape – congratulations!

Round. The round face is usually short and fairly wide. Often has full cheeks leading to a rounded chin.

Heart. The widest part of this face is the forehead which then curves towards a small, neat chin.

Pear. The opposite to the heart shape. This face has a narrower forehead with a broader jawline.

ANGULAR OUTLINES

Rectangle. The face is quite narrow in comparison to its length and is often characterised by a deep forehead and angular jawline.

Square. This face is well defined, with its width and length often being equal. It will often look short and wide with chiselled edges.

Diamond. The diamond shape is characterised by a narrow forehead and chin with exceptionally wide, high cheekbones.

HAIRSTYLE GUIDELINES

CURVED OUTLINES

Oval. You really have the freedom to experiment and try lots of different styles. Centre or side partings will look good. Long or short styles can be equally stunning. If you are petite or have very fine hair, a shorter style will look best. Also, if you are petite, you may want to give yourself an additional inch or two on top with a hairstyle that adds some height.

Round. A round face is always best with a hairstyle which gives some height, to lengthen and slim the face. If your hair is thin or fine or you have difficulty keeping the height on top, a gentle perm or root perm may be the answer. Keep the style soft – an angular cut, because of its conflicting lines, can make the face look fat. Gently curving at the sides with height on top is ideal.

Heart. The heart-shaped face with its wide forehead and narrow chin does not really need any extra width at the top. The wide forehead can be covered with a fringe if desired, but best to keep it minimal and wispy. If you want any volume at all to your hair, the

OVAL

ROUND

DIAMOND

Take your hair back, draw round your face in the mirror and see which shape it resembles.

HEART

PEAR

RECTANGLE

SQUARE

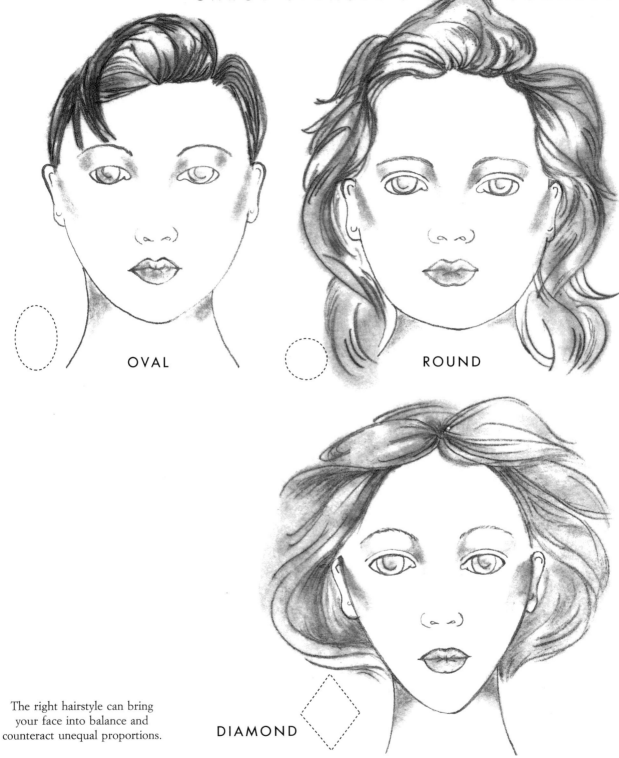

OVAL

ROUND

DIAMOND

The right hairstyle can bring your face into balance and counteract unequal proportions.

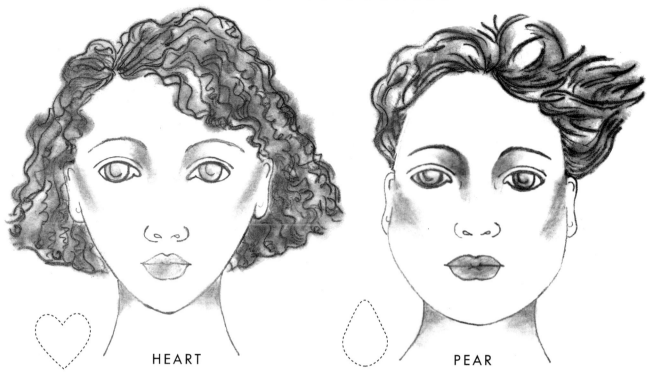

HEART

PEAR

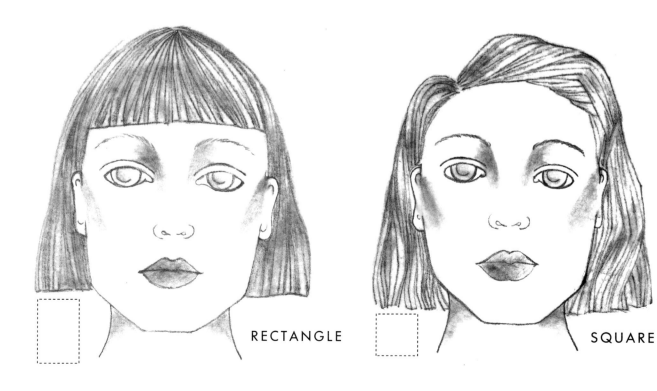

RECTANGLE

SQUARE

best place is around the delicate chin where curls or a soft bob shape look superb.

Pear. As the pear is opposite to the heart, the reverse advice is true! You do not really want to add extra width at your jawline so volume in that area is best avoided. A cascade of curls across the forehead tapering down to wisps at the jawline would be ideal.

ANGULAR OUTLINES

Rectangle. The long, rectangular face will definitely benefit from a fringe to reduce its length. The last thing you need is any extra height on top. Also, very long hair will echo your face shape and emphasise it. A fairly angular cut will look good, as long as it has a fringe of some sort, and width at the sides.

Square. A square face will look less so with an asymmetrical style. The best way to achieve this is with an off-centre parting. As the face is short, a full, heavy fringe is not a good idea. A voluminous style (a perm may be necessary) will look good if the bottom edge is kept angular.

Diamond. The high, wide cheekbones are the greatest asset of this face and should be left on show in all their glory. A style which is fairly short and close to the head around the cheekbones looks wonderful – you wouldn't want to add any extra width at this point. Volume around the forehead and/or the chin area, however, will look good as the bone structure is at its narrowest here.

'I like to think I'm interesting, not beautiful.'

Rosie, age 17

DEFINING YOUR FACIAL CHARACTERISTICS

So far I have only dealt with the *outline* of your face to determine the best *shape* of your hairstyle. But there is more to your face than its outline – you also have features such as eyes, eyebrows, nose, lips and cheeks, all of which have their own individuality and add to your unique look. Some people have quite curved features; others have very angular ones; and some have a mixture of both, but with one type probably dominant.

The angularity or softness of your features, combined with your face outline, will help you choose your most flattering necklines, glasses, jewellery and hats.

Always *accentuate the positive* where angles or curves are concerned – this is what personal style is all about. Be confident about your look. If your face is mostly made up of angles – like Jackie Onassis or Princess Diana – then play this up with angular necklines, jewellery, glasses, etc. If your face is mostly soft curves – like Liz Taylor or Naomi Campbell – have the confidence to complement these features with curved necklines, accessories, hats, etc.

Look in the mirror or study *current* photos of yourself (remember that your characteristics can change as you grow older) or ask a friend or relative to help you assess your features (sometimes it is difficult to assess yourself objectively when you've seen your face a million times). Try to look at your face from all angles, not just from the front – you may be surprised at the reality as seen from the side or off-centre!

First, tick the box below for your closest face shape.

CURVED

1 arched eyebrows
2 rounded eyes
3 soft cheeks
4 rounded nose
5 full mouth

ANGULAR

1 straight eyebrows
2 almond eyes
3 prominent cheekbones
4 sharper nose
5 thin mouth

CURVED OUTLINES				ANGULAR OUTLINES			
OVAL	☐	ROUND	☐	SQUARE	☐	RECTANGLE	☐
HEART	☐	PEAR	☐	DIAMOND	☐		

Then, tick the boxes below for the features resembling your own.

	CURVED FEATURES		ANGULAR FEATURES	
Eyebrows:	ROUNDED/ARCHED	☐	STRAIGHT/SHARP	☐
Cheeks:	SOFT/ROUNDED	☐	PROMINENT BONES	☐
Eyes:	FULL/ROUND	☐	ALMOND	☐
Nose:	ROUNDED/FULL	☐	THIN/STRAIGHT	☐
Lips:	ROUNDED/FULL	☐	THIN/STRAIGHT	☐
Chin:	CURVED/ROUNDED	☐	SQUARE/POINTED	☐

If you have ticked boxes mostly in the 'Curved' column, your face has mostly soft, contoured lines. If you ticked mostly in the 'Angular' column, your face projects a straighter, sharper impression. If you ticked a mixture from both columns, the column with most ticks shows the dominant direction of your features and you are best emphasising these lines to develop your personal style.

Understanding your face outline and its features will now help you to develop the guidelines for your best hairstyle even further. For example, if you have an oval face with mostly angular features you know you have quite a lot of freedom with the style but it would be best to keep the cut sharp and angular. If you have a square face but with mostly curved features, you know your best option would be an asymmetrical style with a side parting; no fringe but lots of softness and curve in the volume to complement your features.

Opposite: Curved features are best complemented by soft frames. Don't be afraid of bold jewellery with glasses, but don't overdo it or you might look like a Christmas tree! With glasses and large earrings it is best to leave off a necklace.

Angular features look best with a sharper style of glasses such as these rectangular frames. Notice also how the straighter hairstyle and neckline work well with the frames.

SPECS APPEAL – GO GET IT!

As glasses sit right on top of your face, they are of equal importance to your hairstyle in achieving your best look. Like hairstyles, people can go horribly wrong with their choice of glasses, yet it really is quite simple to select your most flattering shape of frame.

A high bridge on glasses will lengthen a short or squat nose. The deep colour of the bridge is ideal for bringing wide-set (eg Oriental) eyes together.

Many women fear wearing glasses, thinking they will render them plain and unattractive – perhaps remembering the old adage 'men don't make passes at girls who wear glasses'. Today, nothing could be further from the truth: the dazzling array of colours, shapes and styles available means that glasses can be *the* ultimate fashion accessory and a way of enhancing your looks and expressing your personality.

Glasses no longer linger in the same embarrassing category as Zimmer frames and surgical stockings, so don't buy the cheapest, most boring frames in existence in the hope that no one will notice them – that really is denying the obvious! Just realise what continental Europeans did decades ago: glasses can be incredibly chic and even downright sexy. Why not splash out on a few pairs and have different styles for work, leisure and evening?

GUIDELINES FOR GLASSES

Even if you don't wear glasses now, you may need them in the future, and everyone needs sunglasses for the summer, so the following guidelines will help you choose your best specs ever.

SHAPE OF FRAMES

You already know whether you have a more curved or angular face, so choosing your best shape of frame is now easy. Select glasses with similar angular or curved lines, to complement rather than contrast with your features. However, it is best not to repeat or emphasise your face shape *exactly* with the frame of your glasses:

- A *round* face will not look good in round glasses but will suit gentle ovals, 'softened' squares or swept-up 'cats-eye' styles.
- A *square* face should not echo its shape with square glasses but 'flattened' rectangles will look good.
- The *heart* shape will not want to emphasise the forehead with a heavy top-frame to the glasses. Round styles look good.
- The *pear* shape will not want to emphasise the jawline with bottom-heavy frames. Aviator styles look good.
- The *diamond* shape needs to keep the frames quite close to the

head in order that the cheekbones are not widened further.

- The *rectangular, long* face can take quite large glasses but it is best to keep the frames angular.
- The *oval* face has more freedom again (lucky you!) and is best guided towards angularity or contoured frames by facial features.

SIZE OF FRAMES

For glasses to look balanced on your face, the top of the frame should follow your eyebrows as closely as possible; the sides of the frame should not extend greatly beyond the sides of your face; and the bottom of the frame should not be touching your cheeks.

Glasses which extend above the eyebrow give a 'double-eyebrow' effect and a look of constant surprise; frames which extend beyond the sides of the head give the wearer an uncanny resemblance to 'Brains', the *Thunderbirds* puppet; and glasses which rest too low on the cheek leave the eye 'floating' at the top of the lens like a goldfish surfacing in its bowl.

WEIGHT OF FRAMES

If you are petite or have delicate bone structure, it is easy to look overwhelmed in heavy glasses. A small frame in a lightweight metal or even a 'frameless' style would be very flattering. If you are fuller figured or have heavier bone structure, very small, delicate glasses would look out of place. Opt instead for larger frames in a heavy acetate which would be complementary to your scale.

HATE YOUR NOSE?

A long, thin nose can be shortened by the right glasses – choose ones with a low bridge for a nose job without surgery! Conversely, if you have the flat, 'squashed' variety, a very high bridge will create the illusion of a longer, slimmer nose.

SEEING EYE TO EYE

Wide-set eyes (e.g. Oriental eyes) can be brought closer together with a dark, heavy bridge, while close-set eyes will have more space created between them with a clear, transparent bridge.

'I hold packets at arms length to read them – I'm terrified of wearing glasses.'

Lynne, age 42

Glasses with a low bridge such as these will shorten an over-long or large nose. The transparent bridge is also good for close-set eyes.

If you have curved features, look for jewellery with soft, contoured lines. As well as round, button or hoop earrings, add necklaces and brooches with scroll, swirl or shell designs to your collection.

Angular jewellery is more hard to find, so if you have angular features, snap it up when you see it! As well as square, triangular and rectangular pieces, look also for more creative geometric designs such as this superb 'woven gold' collection.

ACCESSORIES AROUND THE FACE

GUIDELINES FOR JEWELLERY

As with glasses, jewellery looks best if it complements, rather than conflicts with, the angles or contours of the face, but it is better not to repeat the exact face shape in the pieces.

An angular face will look good with jewellery made up of mostly straight lines – square, rectangular, triangular or 'zig-zag' earrings with matching necklaces and brooches.

A softer face is best complemented by jewellery made up of curved lines – round, oval, button or 'hoop' earrings with similar necklaces and brooches.

SELECTING EARRINGS FOR FACE SHAPES

Earrings and Face Shapes – earrings are the closest jewellery to the face and always benefit from a little thought:

Oval – as with hairstyles, you can get away with most earring shapes. Follow the softness or angularity of your features in choosing the best designs.

Round – select earrings which give length rather than width eg ovals, swirls, hoops, drops.

Heart – choose earrings with more width at the bottom than the top eg pear shapes, teardrops, triangles.

Pear – the opposite of the heart, needing a shape with more width at the top and a narrower bottom.

Rectangle – avoid very long, drop designs and choose styles which are short and wide eg squares, buttons.

Diamond – like the heart, you can add width near your narrow chin with pear shapes, teardrops, triangles etc.

GUIDELINES FOR NECKLINES

I will be dealing with clothing in the next chapter of the book, but as necklines are so close to the face, they really belong in this chapter, as they are much more important as the *final* framing pieces to the face. Study the list at the bottom of the page to become familiar with the styles that will best complement your face and choose the ones which appeal to your personality, age or lifestyle.

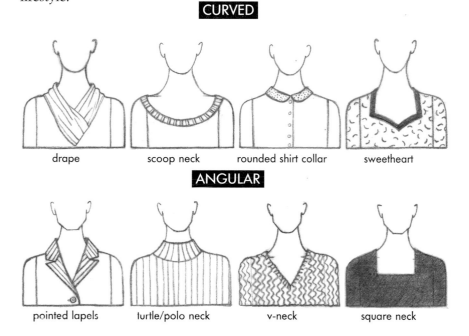

CURVED

drape   scoop neck   rounded shirt collar   sweetheart

ANGULAR

pointed lapels   turtle/polo neck   v-neck   square neck

CURVED NECKLINES		ANGULAR NECKLINES	
cowl neck	rounded shirt collar	turtle/polo neck	v-waterfall
scoop neck	drape	v-neck	pointed shirt collar
sweetheart	curved lapels	square-neck	cross-over
shawl collar	drop-notch lapels	mandarin collar	pointed lapels
pie-crust		wing-collar	peaked lapels
tied/bow			

Chiselled features are set off superbly by angular hats. Look for crisp fabrics, flattish crowns and stiff brims. Don't forget to keep straight lines in your jewellery too.

Some necklines are so plain that they are neither very curved nor angular and therefore suit most people. These are: crew neck, jewel neck, boat neck, T-shirt top and collarless jackets.

When you begin building a wardrobe of complementary necklines you'll find that all your clothes go together. A jacket with rounded lapels teamed with a pointed-collar shirt will not look good, but slip a scoop-neck T-shirt beneath the jacket and it looks fantastic. Top that with a soft hairstyle, curvaceous glasses and a pair of contoured earrings and you're well on the way to developing a consistent personal style.

GUIDELINES FOR HATS

Wearing a hat procures the best tables in restaurants; makes porters suddenly appear out of the gloom of British Rail stations; and on one memorable transatlantic flight, resulted in my ticket being upgraded to first class.

Apart from this wonderful bonus of 'instant respect' that hat-wearing generates, there is the very practical aspect of keeping warm to be considered. A very large percentage of body heat is lost through the head, rendering the hat one of the most useful accessories to have in or, more aptly, on top of, one's wardrobe.

If hats are so good to wear, with practical benefits too, why do most of us only wear them for weddings, christenings and other formal do's, where we invariably look embarrassed and whip them off at the nearest available opportunity? Many women have told me they would like to wear hats more often but haven't a clue how to choose their best style, let alone how to put and keep the !**! thing on once they have bought it!

In the good old days of the Thirties and Forties, the art of successful hat wearing was passed on from mother to daughter – a tradition which seemed to fade away with the emergence of 'the teenager' in the Fifties, who wouldn't be seen dead in anything that mother was wearing. So I will now try to revive those gems of wisdom for the lost generation who have missed out on hat style.

1 *Consider the shape.* You should already know whether you have a soft, contoured face or a sharp angular face. It is best to choose a hat with similar, rather than contrasting lines. A sharp, angular face (eg Jackie Onassis) will suit a pill box or trilby; a more curvaceous face (Liz Taylor) will suit a more floppy style. *Angular* hats have features such as square crowns and flat brims and are generally made with stiffer fabrics with petersham trim and often little decoration. Angular hat pins look good. *Curved* hats have softer features such as rounded crowns and floppy brims and are generally made of more pliable materials with lace or flower trimmings. Rounded hat pins (eg pearl) look best.

A floppy-brimmed hat is the perfect complement to a softly featured face. Look for malleable fabrics, rounded crowns and contoured brims. Cool, curvy pearls complete the perfect picture.

2 *Never sit down to choose a hat.* You must view yourself in a full-length mirror as the hat must be in proportion to the rest of your body. An overweight or large-boned lady needs a substantial hat to prevent it from looking like a pea on a drum! Conversely, a petite or small-boned woman needs a smaller scale of hat so as not to look overpowered and weedy beneath a huge, frothy concoction. All hat departments need full-length mirrors but very rarely have them – therefore, take your selection of hats to the dress department.

3 *Get a good fit.* If the hat fits properly, you should be able to feel the top of your head at the top of the crown, and the sides of the hat should wedge firmly on the sides of the head. When looking straight-on into a mirror, the crown should be as wide as the *widest* part of the face and the brim should not be wider than the shoulders. Hats should not be precariously balanced on top of the head and should not blow off with the first puff of wind. If the hat has a deep crown and is a good fit, you should be able to hold your head upside down without it falling off. Stylish, fashionable hats without a deep crown have to do more of a balancing act but should be secured with hat pins (now coming back into fashion) or with elastic (not under the chin!) beneath the hair at the nape of the neck. Always keep a note of your hat size for future purchases.

4 *Consider your hairstyle.* A very full hairstyle makes it difficult to wear a hat. For formal occasions, long, full hair looks best tied back, plaited or put up inside a hat with a full crown. Take the hat to your hairdresser so that he or she can help you achieve the desired result. Some more casual hats – eg berets, straw hats – can look good with long hair, but the general rule for formal hats is to show as little hair as possible. Short, neat haircuts are therefore the easiest for hat wearing. If you do leave long hair down, keep your outfit as simple as possible.

5 *Select the best colour.* To get a lot of wear out of a hat, it is best to choose one in a neutral colour (see Chapter 6 for best neutral colours). Then it will go with all your coats, jackets, suits, etc. For a special occasion you can always dress it up or match it to the colour of your outfit with coloured ribbon, flowers, etc. If you want to have a matching hat and outfit in *exactly* the same colour, always buy the outfit first and then take it along to the hat shop/department to ensure a good match – never try to 'remember' a colour, as a mismatch of hat and dress can look disastrous. Too much 'matching', however, can look contrived and very amateurish, eg navy dress with red hat, red belt, red shoes and red handbag can look overdone. Much more stylish to have the accent colour only twice, eg navy dress, navy hat with red flower/ribbon, red belt, navy bag and shoes.

6 *Brim with confidence.* So now you've selected your best style, fit and colour of hat, you have to ensure that you put it on and successfully 'angle' the hat to create the desired stunning effect, as seen on the catwalks and in the Royal Enclosure at Ascot. Quite simply, you pull the hat right down to the eyebrows, feel the head in the top of the crown, and then tip the hat slightly to the left or right. If the hat is on correctly, you will not be able to see anything! You therefore have to lift your head to see where you are going – which elongates your neck, puts your shoulders back and makes you, and the hat, look wonderful.

'I'd love to wear hats more often but no-one else seems to.'

Patricia, age 50

CHAPTER TWO

STRAIGHT UP-AND-DOWN OR ALL IN-AND-OUT

*F*OR YOUR CLOTHES to look good on you and for you to feel comfortable and confident in them, they need to fit perfectly and look as though they were made for you. Not many of us enjoy the luxury of a made-to-measure wardrobe, but by reaching a full understanding of your body – with all its lumps and bumps; good points and not so good points – you can achieve that perfect look from off-the-peg clothes.

Your

> '*I'm straight up-and-down whereas I'd like to be in-and-out!*'
>
> *Angela, age 38*

Many style consultants, and books on the subject, divide women's bodies into half a dozen or so shapes – round, pear, triangle, etc – and give advice accordingly. Women's bodies, however, are not that simple or similar! It may be possible to do that for faces, as they are relatively small objects – only ⅛th of your total body size. Your body, however, covers a much bigger area and a multitude of sins!

One 'pear-shaped' woman, for example, may be short with a small bust and slim waist; her 'pear-shaped' sister may be tall with a large bust and no waistline. It would be ridiculous to give them *exactly* the same style guidelines just because they both happen to have shoulders smaller than their bottom halves.

Your body is unique; it is made up of the total sum of all your different body proportions. Just as I didn't stop at simply analysing your face outline, but also took into account your unique facial features (which very few consultants do), in the next chapter I will not only address your body outline, but will also show you how to

figure

dress to balance any proportional problems you may have. First of all, however, you need to assess whether you are 'straight up-and-down' or 'all in-and-out'.

DEFINING YOUR BODY OUTLINE

It's time to get the mirror out again – this time a full-length one. The process may not be as messy as analysing your face shape, but you may find it more painful as, I'm afraid, you need to look at yourself, straight on, in your underwear, swimsuit or leotard, or even in the 'altogether' if you feel confident enough!

You need to look only at your body's *exterior* outline – put your arms slightly away from your sides to do this and keep your legs together. Ignore for the moment whether you have a flat chest, or large tummy or prominent backside (these are proportional issues, which I will deal with in the next chapter).

- *Your shoulders* – are they broad and straight or more narrow and sloping?
- *Your ribcage/midriff* – is it wide and straight or more narrow and tapered toward your waist?
- *Your waist* – is it clearly visible as an indentation or is there little difference between your ribs and hips?
- *Your hips/thighs* – do they flare out from your waistline or continue on straight down from your waist?
- *Your calves* – are they curved and tapered towards your ankle or straighter in shape all the way down?

Tick the boxes on the facing page to find out whether your body has a straighter outline or a more more curved outline. There are two very important things to mention here:

Tick the following boxes with your answers:

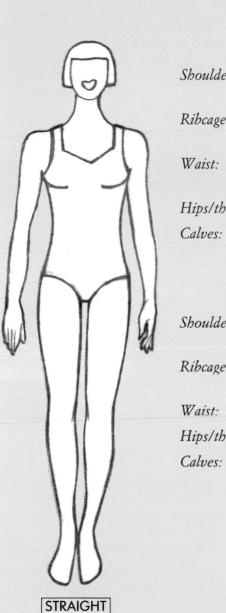

STRAIGHT

	STRAIGHT OUTLINE	
Shoulders:	STRAIGHT AND/OR BROAD	☐
Ribcage:	WIDE AND/OR STRAIGHT	☐
Waist:	INVISIBLE/BARELY THERE	☐
Hips/thighs:	LOW/FLATTER	☐
Calves:	FLATTER/STRAIGHT	☐

	CURVED OUTLINE	
Shoulders:	NARROW AND/OR SLOPING	☐
Ribcage:	NARROW AND/OR TAPERED	☐
Waist:	CLEARLY VISIBLE	☐
Hips/thighs:	HIGH/ROUNDED	☐
Calves:	CURVED/TAPERED	☐

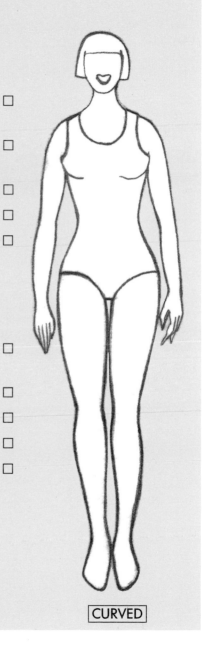

CURVED

YOUR FIGURE

STRAIGHT

A straight outline is still feminine! In fact, most of the world's supermodels have quite straight bodies – straight shoulders, broad ribcages, little waist evidence, and flat hips and thighs. What I have dealt with so far is mostly based on your inherited bone structure. All the added appendages – bust, stomach, bottom, etc – are what can make this shape very feminine indeed.

CURVED

A curved outline does not mean fat! People always seem to associate curves with fat but this is not necessarily so. You can be very slim and fit and still have a curved body outline. In fact, the majority of very overweight women have a straight body outline – their shoulders become wider, their ribcage and waists thicken and their thighs and calves get heavier and straighter.

So, remember – a straight body outline can be slim (Princess Diana) or fuller-figured (Queen Elizabeth). A curved outline can also be slim (Madonna) or fuller-figured (Roseanne). Putting on or losing a few pounds here and there will not change your body outline dramatically. A curved body outline needs to put on several stone to become straighter. No amount of dieting, however, will give a skinny waist to a straight body with a wide ribcage. Exercise a straighter body to keep hips and thighs as slim as possible, while building up the shoulders to create the illusion of a slimmer waist – as Princess Diana has done to great effect over recent years.

GUIDELINES FOR SELECTING CLOTHING SHAPES

This really couldn't be simpler. If you are straighter in the body, straighter garments will make you look good and feel comfortable. If you are more curved in the body, straighter clothing will not fit so well or make you look good, whereas more contoured styles will look fantastic. Can you imagine Madonna in a double-breasted,

straight blazer that would look stunning on Princess Diana? Or a belted, peplum jacket on Martina Navratilova (straight body), perhaps borrowed from Raquel Welch (curved body). The answer in both cases is obviously, no!

That is why you should never buy something because it looks good on someone else or on a model in a magazine. Very often the reason it looks good on that woman is because *she* is in it! How depressing it is in the changing room when you try on a garment which can be your correct size, only to see a horrendous sight in the mirror. It could be hanging off the shoulder, too loose in the waist, stretched around your hips, stomach and bottom, etc. The reason for this is because it is the *wrong shape*; not necessarily the wrong size.

If only Princess Diana had known what she knows today about her shape when planning her wedding dress many years ago. Although a beautiful, fairy tale dress, it was not right for her in any way – a fact she recently confided to a dinner companion in New York. The flounces on her broad shoulders only made them seem wider; the soft neckline did nothing for her angular face (neither did the soft hairstyle); and the gathers of the skirt came out from her wide ribcage. If she were to marry again (who knows!), she would choose a very different gown: angular neckline to complement her angular face and now angular hairstyle; plain shoulders; a long, straight bodice skimming past her waistline; and any fullness starting lower down near her slim hips/thighs.

Study the following lists for your straight or curved body outline to obtain a good idea of the kind of 'silhouette' of clothing you need to look for when you go shopping. In any fashion season, there are always straighter and more curved styles to choose from. Now you will be able to select *your* most flattering styles successfully, year after year.

Remember to bear your face in mind too by selecting tops/jackets/dresses, etc with *your* kind of neckline. Obviously, you do not need to take your face into account when selecting the bottom half of your clothing (skirts, trousers, shorts, etc) – only your body outline is important then.

> '*Some women look good in everything – I have to try really hard.*'
>
> *Vivienne, age 40*

Near left: Princess Diana has learned over the years how to dress her straighter figure to best effect. Angular necklines, straight jackets and skirts and a short, sharp hairstyle have become the signature of her style.

Above: Nice dress, wrong body! What Princess Diana didn't need on her wedding were frills and flounces on her wide shoulders, a soft hairstyle and neckline, and a full skirt starting at her wide ribcage. Choosing her wedding dress today, she would probably opt for a V or mandarin neckline, plain shoulders and a straight bodice skimming past her waistline with any fullness starting near her slimmer hip-line.

Far left: Elizabeth Taylor uses her curves to best advantage; always a soft hairstyle to complement her heart-shaped face and fitted dresses or suits with curved necklines and plenty of waist emphasis.

JACKETS

STRAIGHT	CURVED
Look for:	Look for:

STRAIGHT	CURVED
■ Little or no waist emphasis	■ Waist emphasis – fitted styles
■ Tailored lines	■ Belted jackets
■ Tightly woven fabrics	■ Curved seams
■ Little or no texture	■ Soft tailoring
■ Well-defined seams	■ Softly woven fabrics
■ Top-stitching	■ No top-stitching, or fine top-stitching
■ Crisp straight closings	
■ Well-defined shoulders/ square pads	■ Single-breasted or centre-button fastenings
■ Few darts	■ Darted bustlines
■ Straight or angular hemlines	■ Soft shoulder pads
■ Well-defined pockets – square, piped, slashed	■ Rounded hemlines
	■ Flap, rounded or set-in pockets

TOPS
(SHIRTS, SWEATERS, WAISTCOATS ETC)

STRAIGHT	CURVED
Look for:	Look for:

STRAIGHT	CURVED
■ Safari-style shirts	■ Fitted shirts
■ Chanel-style cardigans	■ Draw-string waists
■ Men's-style shirts	■ Belted blouses
■ Cable sweaters/cardigans	■ Crochet sweaters
■ Straight twin-sets	■ Belted/cropped twin-sets
■ Ribbed sweaters	■ Fitted waistcoats
■ Straight waistcoats	■ Flared gilets
■ Straight gilets	■ Surplice-style tops
■ Indo-Chine-style tunics	■ Bodies
■ Camisole top	■ Bustiers

CAROL SPENSER'S STYLE COUNSEL

BOTTOMS
(SKIRTS, TROUSERS, SHORTS ETC)

STRAIGHT

Look for:

- Straight skirts
- Tailored lines/tightly woven fabrics
- Pressed down/stitched down pleats
- Straight wrapover skirts
- Straight or gently tapered trousers
- Pockets – well defined, square, piped, slashed
- Straight jeans
- Tailored city-shorts/culottes
- Safari-style shorts
- Straight palazzos

CURVED

Look for:

- Tapered skirts
- Soft lines/softly woven fabrics
- Soft, unpressed pleats/ gathers
- Gored/flared skirts/sarong wrapovers
- Tapered trousers
- 'Paper-bag'-waist trousers/ shorts
- Skorts (flared shorts)
- Flap, rounded or set-in pockets
- Easy-fit/relaxed fit jeans
- Flowing palazzos

DRESSES

STRAIGHT

Look for:

- Straight slip
- Shift dress – Sixties style
- Shirt waister
- Drop waist
- Straight dress
- Sweater dress
- Straight pinafore
- Two piece – blouse outside
- Straight evening gown

CURVED

Look for:

- Fitted slip
- Tea-dress – Forties style
- Wrap-over style
- Fitted waist
- Fitted coat-dress
- Fitted sheath
- Fitted pinafore
- Two piece – blouse on inside
- Skirted evening gown

STRAIGHT SELECT CLOTHING WITH LITTLE WAIST EMPHASIS
FOR A STRAIGHTER FIGURE

CURVED SELECT CLOTHING WITH SHAPE AND MOVEMENT
FOR THE CURVED FIGURE

COATS

STRAIGHT	CURVED
Look for:	Look for:

STRAIGHT — Look for:

- Tailored topstitching
- Well-defined pockets
- Straight hems
- Trench coat (tie belt at back if wide waisted)
- Crombie-style
- Unconstructed
- Edge-to-edge
- Duffle coat
- Car coat
- Straight parka

CURVED — Look for:

- Softly tailored/little or no topstitching
- Curved, flap or set-in pockets
- Curved/flowing hemlines
- Swing raincoat
- Swagger coat
- Fitted waist
- Princess line
- Bath-robe style (belted)
- Belted trench
- Drawstring parka

SELECTING FABRIC

You may have clothes in your wardrobe which you rarely or never war because they don't 'feel right'. The following tips on fabric may be useful:

Drapey fabrics – ideal for curvy figures as they hang well on contoured shapes. They are slimming as they can be made up into garments with few seams or darts. Drapey fabric is good for a fuller figure if it is medium-weight and not too floaty.

Stiff fabrics – good for the slim, straight figure. Stiff crisp fabrics are not recommended for a fuller figure as seams or darts can add bulk to the body.

Texture – bulky, nubbly, ribbed, fleeced fabrics add bulk to the body and are best avoided by the petite or fuller-figured.

Sheen – shiny fabrics reflect the light and make the body look bigger. Matt fabrics absorb light and reduce the size of the body.

Colour – light colours attract the eye, reflect the light and expand the object they cover.

LOWER BODY ACCESSORIES

As belts and bags are worn or carried very close to your body, it will always look better if they complement your body outline and clothing just as jewellery, necklines, hats and glasses complemented your face.

STRAIGHT

- Briefcase – hard leather
- Handbag – boxy style with angular clasp – eg 'Kelly bag'
- Shoulder bag – rectangular shape
- Evening bag – clutch or envelope style
- Tote bag – crisp fabric, eg straw
- Back pack – angular design and buckles
- Belt – hard leather and angular buckles

STRAIGHT

If you are straight in the body and also have a fuller figure with a wide waistline, it is wise not to draw attention to your middle with an obvious belt. Best to wear long straight tops which bypass your waistline altogether. If you have a straight, slim body, you can create more of a waistline with an attractive belt if you want to.

CURVED

- Briefcase – soft leather, satchel style
- Handbag – rounded, contoured clasp
- Shoulder bag – drawstring leather
- Evening bag – velvet 'pouch' style
- Clutch – oval, clasp-top style
- Tote bag – soft fabric, eg string, crochet
- Back pack – pouchy design, rounded buckles
- Belts – soft leather and curved buckles

CURVED

CHAPTER THREE

PROPORTIONS THROUGHOUT HISTORY

THERE IS NO such thing as the perfect body – only the image that society deems is perfect at any moment in time. Throughout history – and even today in different parts of the world – the 'perfect' female body varies enormously. The influences on such ideals and indeed on fashion itself, as the two go hand in hand, are many and varied and stem from the cultural, social and even political atmosphere of the time.

'My problem is that I was born in the wrong era.'

Denise, age 45

This has been the case since time began, when man and woman donned the first animal skin, painted their faces with mud, and used sticks and stones as jewellery. But if we look at just the twentieth century in the so-called 'civilised', western societies, we can see how many times the 'ideal' female form has been reinvented to suit the mood of the times:

- **At the turn of the century**, when women were mere chattels of men, sloping shoulders (which signal weakness) and large hips and stomach (indicating fertility) reduced men to quivering wrecks. Being plump was desirable as this signalled wealth. Women wore padding and bustles to emphasise their lower portions. Lily-white skin was envied as this meant you were a lady-of-leisure who spent her time indoors; a sun-tan marked you as one of the lower classes who worked outdoors.

- **In the Twenties and Thirties**, women were striving for liberation and equality with men. This resulted in a more 'masculine'

proportions

VICTORIAN   **TWENTIES/THIRTIES**   **FORTIES**

female form becoming the most envied. Broad shoulders were now in vogue, and women bound their breasts to achieve a flat chest. Waistlines, hips and stomachs were not at all important and all dresses became straight and shapeless. When not in dresses, women wore trousers for the first time in an attempt to ape men's style, which also included smoking cigarettes, driving cars and playing golf!

FIFTIES   **SIXTIES**   **SEVENTIES**

■ **The war years of the Forties** had a big impact on the way women looked. As the men went off to war and the women took over in the factories, offices and fields, big shoulders on a woman signalled capability and strength – shoulder padding for jackets was in big demand. Women often became the sole providers – the male and female parent to their children – and their look mirrored this. Their bodies became split almost in two parts: the top all bulky, masculine and strong; with a tiny, feminine waist and rounded hips and bottom wiggling in a tight skirt beneath! As cloth was in short supply, skirts became short for the first time, and so, also for the first time, shapely calves became important. Only ankles had been visible before this time!

■ **In the Fifties**, a woman's place was back in the home, looking after the returned heroes and having babies to boost the lost population – you only have to read the women's magazines of this time to get that message loud and clear. Sloping shoulders were back, displayed in off-the-shoulder blouses. Breasts became very important and bra-engineering was invented to give women the best uplift ever. Curvy, 'child-bearing' hips and rounded stomachs were considered sexy. Women were being cared for by men again, like children – even to the point where grown women wore ponytails, frilly petticoats and ankle socks.

■ **The advent of 'the pill' in the Sixties** gave women sexual freedom and prompted the movement for equality and liberation to rise again. As in the Twenties and Thirties, the ideal female form became androgynous – straight shoulders, flat chests, no waistline, flat hips, stomach and thighs. Because of the huge technological advances in fabric manufacture, the look, however, was very difficult: nylon shift dresses, straight PVC macs and even chain-link tabards. For the first time this century, everyone had enough to eat, so looking well-fed meant nothing. Dieting began and every woman tried to turn herself into the world's first supermodel, Twiggy.

■ **The generation of the Seventies** rejected the materialism, excesses and overt consumerism of the Sixties and turned to more spiritual matters – love, peace and getting stoned! Eastern influences on women's appearance were strong – long flowing hair coloured with henna; voluminous kaftans came as a great relief to those who had not managed to get 'stick-thin' in the decade before; and all those old symbols of fertility, breasts, hips and stomachs, came back into fashion. The older generation opted for the romantic English look epitomised by Laura Ashley.

■ **The Eighties were 'boom' years** economically, with women being encouraged to buy houses, start businesses, and combine motherhood with a career. 'Superwoman' had arrived, who, as in the Forties, took the world once more on her shoulders, needing those big shoulder-pads again to do it. Beneath that padding, however, there were no curvy hips, stomach and bottom allowed this time – now you had to enrol at the gym or sweat to an exercise video to keep all areas below the waist as tight and flat as possible, while building up those capable shoulders!

■ **The Nineties** have seen women finally achieve image freedom – they have come a long way since the beginning of the century and will no longer be pressured into a look which does not suit their individuality.

In past decades, most women tried to conform to the 'ideal' whatever their body outline or proportions. Today you can choose, from a myriad different styles in the shops, the ones which are perfect for you – Thirties trouser suits, Forties tea-dresses, Fifties capri-pants, Sixties shift dresses, Seventies ethnic styles, Eighties 'power suits'. The list is endless as all past fashions merge into one glorious mix – even the Victorian bustle made an appearance recently on the Paris catwalks!

Each fashion season (twice yearly), I, and my international colleagues publish a comprehensive *Fashion Portfolio* detailing all the current themes, clothing and accessories available in the shops. To help you choose from the overwhelming array of styles in the fashion world today, the garments are all marked to show which type of figure they will flatter most (see page 160 for details of ordering).

'My legs are my best feature; I hate long skirts.'

Kelly, age 27

ANALYSING YOUR PROPORTIONS

You already know, from the previous chapter, the outline of clothes which will be your most flattering, (ie straighter or more curved). I will now show you how to make adjustments to that basic outline to make the most of your proportions in any fashion season.

Tick the boxes below for your own proportions:

BROAD SHOULDERS	☐	NARROW OR SLOPING SHOULDERS	☐
LONG OR THIN NECK	☐	SHORT NECK OR DOUBLE CHIN	☐
SMALL OR NO BUST	☐	LARGE BUST	☐
LONG WAISTED	☐	SHORT WAISTED	☐
FLAT HIPS/STOMACH/ BOTTOM/THIGHS	☐	LARGE HIPS/STOMACH/ BOTTOM/THIGHS	☐
THIN CALVES OR ANKLES	☐	THICK CALVES OR ANKLES	☐
TOO THIN/ UNDERWEIGHT	☐	TALL (OVER 5'9") OR LONG LEGS	☐
PETITE (UNDER 5'3") OR SMALL BONED	☐	FULLER FIGURE OR LARGE BONED	☐

Note: you do not have to tick a box on each line. Only tick the problems which are of concern to you. Then number those concerns in order of importance, with 1 being most important. Should the advice given for one figure concern conflict with that of another, *take the advice for the concern which is most troublesome to you*.

BROAD SHOULDERS

WEAR:

- Small or no shoulder pads – not necessary
- Halter necks – great for swimsuits or dresses
- Raglan sleeves – the seam lessens the shoulders
- V or scoop-necks – (depending on your face) - the depth of the neckline lessens the width of your shoulders
- Thin, spaghetti-straps on swimsuits, dresses and nighties

AVOID:

- Large epaulettes – which make shoulders more noticeable
- Details at shoulder, eg gathers, pleats, stripes, yokes
- Wide/slash necklines
- Broad, wide-set straps on swimsuits, dresses and nighties
- Brooches pinned wide on the shoulder

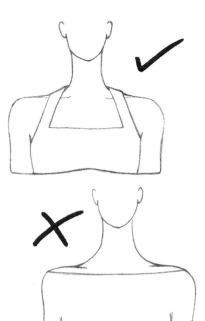

NARROW OR SLOPING SHOULDERS

WEAR:

- Shoulder pads – angular or soft, depending on body outline
- Cap sleeves, which flare out from the shoulder
- Boat or slash necklines
- Horizontal details at shoulders, eg epaulettes/ stripes
- Gathers, pleats, yokes at or near shoulders
- Wide-set, thick straps on swimsuits, evening dresses, sundresses and nighties

AVOID:

- Raglan sleeves – the seam emphasises the slope or narrowness
- Halter necks – the halter emphasises the slope or narrowness
- Puff sleeves – the height of the puff emphasises the slope
- Very low V or scoop-necklines without shoulder pads
- Brooches worn on the lapel or near bust – keep them wide

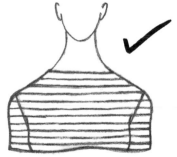

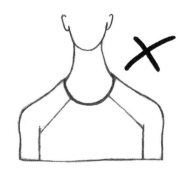

LONG OR THIN NECK

WEAR:

- Scarves tied highly at neckline to suit your face
- Necklines with bows, ties, pie-crust collar
- Choker-style necklaces
- Polo and turtle necks
- Mandarin and Nehru collars

AVOID:

- Very low necklines – fill with scarf or jewellery
- Open shirts and blouses – button quite high
- Scarves tied at a low point
- Very long necklaces – unless layered with shorter ones
- Collarless jackets without a garment beneath

SHORT NECK OR DOUBLE CHIN

WEAR:

- V or scoop-necklines – depending on your face
- Open collars – give illusion of longer, slimmer neck
- Scarves tied low – don't clutter the neck area
- Long necklaces – take the eye downwards
- Collarless jackets worn alone

AVOID:

- High necklines – bows, ties, pie-crust, etc
- Choker-style necklaces – which draw attention to the neck
- Scarves tied high – this emphasises the problem
- Polo and turtle necks – these widen short necks
- Mandarin and Nehru-style collars

SMALL OR NO BUST

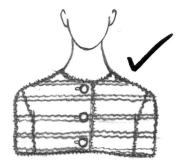

WEAR:

- Bulky textures on top – to add substance
- Horizontal lines/seams at bustline – to increase width
- Layering, eg cropped waistcoats over big shirt
- Breast pockets – add detail at bustline
- Loose-fitting top garments
- Uplift/padded bra

AVOID:

- Very low neckline – shows lack of cleavage!
- Vertical stripes on top – have unwanted slimming effect
- Very tight top (eg bodies) – shows what you have not got!
- High-waisted styles – draws attention up to bust level
- Tank-style swimsuits – support ones are better

LARGE BUST

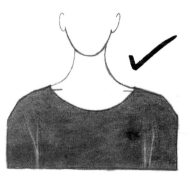

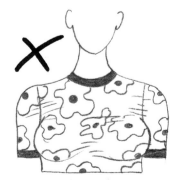

WEAR:

- Plain, matt fabrics on top
- Medium-length necklaces or brooches on shoulder
- Dolman sleeves
- Loose-fitting garments on top
- Vertical or diagonal details on top garments

AVOID:

- Large patterns on top
- Horizontal details across bustline
- Breast pockets, particularly with buttons!
- High-waisted styles
- Tightly fitting tops
- Very long scarves and necklaces which dangle over the precipice!
- Shiny fabrics on top
- Brooches on lapel

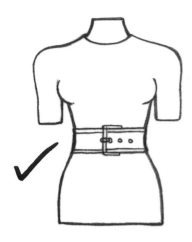

LONG WAISTED
(ie long distance between bust and waist)

WEAR:
- Empire styles
- Wide belts and cummerbunds
- High-waisted styles of skirts and trousers
- Belts in the same colour as the bottom garment
- Contrasting belts or sashes

AVOID:
- Yokes on skirts
- Dropped waist styles
- Garments without waistbands
- Very thin belts
- Hipster styles

SHORT WAISTED
(ie short or no distance between bust and waist)

WEAR:
- Uplift bra to lengthen the midriff
- Garments without waistbands
- Thin belts
- Hipster styles
- Belts in the same colour as the top garment
- Blouses worn outside or 'bloused-out' over bottom garment

AVOID:
- Wide belts and cummerbunds
- High waisted styles of skirts and trousers
- Contrasting belts
- Top garments tucked in tightly
- Poorly fitting bra giving low bust

FLAT HIPS/STOMACH/BOTTOM/THIGHS

WEAR:

- Horizontal details below waist
- Patch pockets on jackets, skirts, trousers
- Short skirts and short shorts
- Cropped jackets and tops
- Gathered waistbands or unsewn pleats
- Long shoulder bags
- Shiny fabrics, patterns and light colours on bottom half

AVOID:

- Vertical lines on bottom half
- Stitched-down pleats
- Very tight clothing on lower half (if very skinny!)
- Shoulders being too wide – avoid pads, epaulettes, etc
- Centre pleats on skirts

LARGE HIPS/STOMACH/BOTTOM/THIGHS

WEAR:

- Shoulder pads (if necessary) or horizontal detail on shoulders to balance bottom half
- Solid deep colours on bottom half
- Prints, lighter or brighter colours on top
- Control briefs and tights
- Vertical stripes and seams on bottom garments
- Stitched-down pleats and eased waistbands
- Matt fabrics on bottom half
- Culotte-style shorts
- Scarves, jewellery to draw attention upwards

AVOID:

- Dangly shoulder bags
- Gathered ankles
- Pockets on lower garments
- Very short skirts and shorts
- Light or shiny fabrics below the waist
- Jackets/tops ending across widest point
- Prints or patterned skirts, trousers and leggings
- Horizontal details on lower half
- Tightly fitting lower garments (beware VPL – Visible Panty Line!)

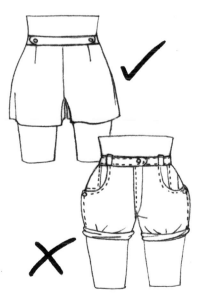

THIN CALVES AND/OR ANKLES

WEAR:

- Light hosiery
- Shiny hosiery
- Delicate shoes and sandals
- Thin ankle straps and T-bar shoes
- Cropped trousers, calf-length Capri pants, leggings
- Calf- or ankle-length skirts

AVOID:

- Clumpy, thick soles
- Too-dark hosiery
- Heavy-heeled shoes and thick ankle straps
- Wide, baggy, knee-length boots
- Ill-fitting ankle boots (legs can look like a mop in a bucket!)

THICK CALVES AND/OR ANKLES

WEAR:

- Deeper, matt hosiery
- Substantial soles and heels
- Darker coloured shoes and boots
- Toning tights and shoes
- Knee-length boots
- Flat, broadly strapped sandals
- Knee- or below-knee length skirts
- Stirrup trousers

AVOID:

- Pale, shiny tights
- Delicate strappy shoes and sandals
- Thin spindly heels
- Calf-length or ankle boots (unless tights match boots)
- Calf-length trousers or Capri pants
- Calf-length skirts
- Leggings

TALL (OVER 5'9") OR LONG LEGS

WEAR:
- Horizontal details
- Layering
- Knee-length skirts
- Different bands of colour/ contrasting belts
- Dropped-yoke on skirts
- Border designs on skirts/ dresses
- Medium to low heels
- Wide trousers and palazzos
- Contrasting tights and shoes
- Turn-ups on trousers

AVOID:
- Vertical lines – stripes, seams, cables, etc
- Dressing in one colour
- Matching tights and skirts
- Very short or very long skirts
- Very slim trousers
- High heels

Tall: try horizontal layers to arrest the eye at intervals down the body. Dress in different blocks of colour, or use contrasting tops, bottoms, legs and shoes.

TOO THIN/UNDERWEIGHT

WEAR:
- Loose clothing
- Layering
- Short hair with some volume
- Horizontal details
- Light-coloured fabrics
- Light hosiery
- Small- to medium-scale patterns
- High necklines
- Small- to medium-scale accessories

AVOID:
- Very tight clothes – eg bodies, leggings
- Vertical lines
- Over-sized accessories
- Long, dangly bags, jewellery, etc
- Long, voluminous hair
- Heavy footwear
- Solid, deep colours
- Open collars and necklines

PETITE AND FULLER FIGURE
(SEE CHAPTER 4)

Underweight: look for substance and texture in your clothing eg loose garments, nubbly or ribbed effects, horizontal details, patch pockets.

ONE-PIECE WONDERS

1

2

1. Dark top slims a big bust. Underwired cups support a large bust (and boost a small one). Vertical stripes slim the torso. No waist detail is good for short-waisted. Low-cut leg conceals big hips.

2. Halter-neck slims down big shoulders. Horizontal centre band emphasises a slim waist and is good for long-waisted. High-cut sides lengthen the legs for petites.

CHOOSING SWIMWEAR

The one place where your vital statistics are put on display, and where it is *very* difficult to hide and balance your figure's problem areas with shoulder pads or wide belts, is the beach. It is therefore essential to choose a swimsuit with the best cut, pattern and fabric to make the most of your good points and draw attention from your worst.

BIKINI OR ONE-PIECE?

My advice on the beach front for any woman who can pinch more than an inch is that a bikini is bad news. The good news for those of us with more than one midriff (and who would rather keep that fact under wraps) is that the one-piece is still a fashionable alternative – annually accounting for 60 percent of all swimsuit sales.

A clever way of achieving the bare-midriff look whilst still

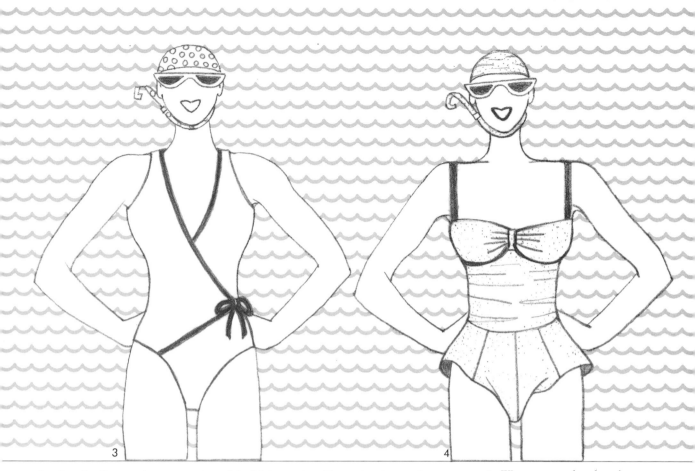

3

4

having it discreetly covered and held in a vice-like grip, is to choose a swimsuit with a tight mesh centre panel or a series of lycra bands on a sheer background. Swimsuits with just the side panels missing, leaving the front and back lycra panels still firmly in place, are ideal if you have a nice waistline but want to keep the tummy well under control. Attention can be focused on the midriff without exposing any flesh at all by choosing designs with ruched, wrap-over, or knotted/tied effects just below the bustline.

UNDERWIRED SUITS

If you don't want to make your midriff the focus of attention you could always go for a well-sculpted, deeply dramatic cleavage. If nature was not too generous to you in this department, there are lots of swimsuits available with 'push-up' wires and padding (sometimes removable). Underwired suits are good for large bosoms to give support and for small ones to create more cleavage.

3. Wrap-over style takes the eye away from a large bust. Shelf-bra gives good support. Tie-side gives waist emphasis – remove bow if wide-waisted. Diagonal line across stomach slims tummy and hips.

4. Wide-set straps broaden narrow shoulders and balance big hips/thighs. Ruched centre detail emphasises waist. Skirt effect hides hip and tummy problems. Underwired cups support a big bust and boost a small one.

TWO-PIECE WONDERS

1. Halter-neck slims broad shoulders. Underwired cups enhance large or small bust. High-cut sides lengthen legs for petites.

2. Ruched, bandeau-style top ideal for boosting small busts. Dark bottom slims large hips, bum and tum. Optional belt features emphasise a small waist – remove if wide-waisted. Low-cut leg flattens big hips.

TIE STRAPS

An equally feminine look (but strictly for the ultra-thin who require no bra support at all) can be achieved with the spaghetti-strap swimsuits which tie prettily on top of the shoulders. Bikini versions are also available with matching string effects at hip level. These styles have returned with the emergence of a modern Nineties 'glam' look – also evident in the strong presence of shiny gold and silver swimsuits and the predominance of 'metallic' appliqué on many designs.

FABRIC CHOICE

Shiny fabrics, however, reflect light and increase the size of the object they cover – particularly stomachs, bottoms and bosoms. So steer clear of metallics and opt for plain matt cotton fabrics if you are a little larger than average. Deep muted patterns such as

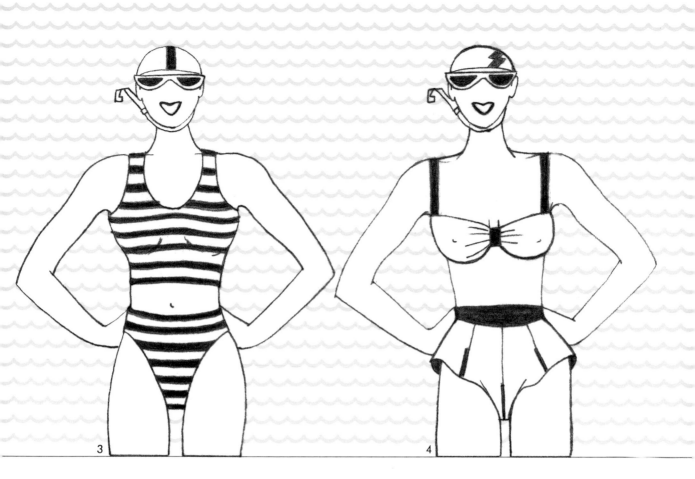

3

4

paisleys, tartans and primitive or animal-skin inspired prints in rich, deep tones can also be slimming. Look out for complementary beach cover-ups – shirts, sarongs, drawstring pants, dresses – in equally matt fabrics such as sand-washed silk, and similarly deep muted patterns.

'ACTIVE' SWIMSUITS

For those who prefer to be active rather than decorative on the beach, there are plenty of 'sportive' styles to choose from. Mainly in black or white (or stripy combinations of day-glo colours), these suits contain a high lycra content in designs featuring wide shoulder straps, tank-style tops and high-waisted shorts-style bottoms. One-piece suits of different cuts and in different colours can be worn over each other for extra support as well as helping to achieve a fashionable 'layered' look.

3. Tank-style bikini for the slim athletic figure. No bust support for small-chested but horizontal stripes give illusion of more width. High-cut legs for flat thighs only!

4. Wide-set straps to broaden narrow shoulders and balance big hips. Underwired top for small or big bust. Waistband emphasises small waist. Skirted bottom hides hip, tum or bum problems.

HOW TO LOOK 10LB SLIMMER IN A SWIMSUIT

1 One-piece suit
2 Deep, muted colour/
   pattern
3 Matt fabric
4 Medium-cut leg (not too
   high or too low)
5 High lycra/spandex
   content
6 Vertical details (stripes,
   seams, buttons, etc)
7 Built-in tummy control
   panel
8 Under-wired bra
9 Wide-set straps
10 Lowish neckline (V or
   sweetheart)

GET FITTED

Bearing in mind all the uncomfortable places that sand can get into whilst you are lazing on a beach, the last thing you need is an ill-fitting swimsuit. If your costume doesn't fit well, it won't ever look or feel right, so always begin with choosing the right size – *usually one size larger than your dress size*. If, for example, you cannot fit your thumbs comfortably under the straps of your costume, or if it bulges, cuts or rides up, it is definitely too small. The real acid test (which may cause a disturbance in the fitting rooms but is still worth doing) is to jump up and down, twist, bend, reach, squat and then see if the swimsuit is still where it's supposed to be . . .

LOOKING BETTER BY DESIGN

The right design of swimsuit can help hide, minimise or emphasise:

■ *Hiding hips* – choose styles that pull the eye upwards with colour and pattern on top and matt colour in the hip area. Look for tied sides, skirted looks and side panels.

■ *Minimise stomach* – fool the eye with fabric or styling that pulls the eye away from the tummy. Look for diagonal stripes, high-waisted bikinis, blouson styles, control panels to hold the midriff.

■ *Full bosom* – needs comfort, support, coverage and details which camouflage or draw the eye away from the bustline. Look for underwired or boned bra-tops; pattern, draping and details at the waist or below; substantial straps. Darker colours on top.

■ *Small bosom* – needs lots of horizontal emphasis to enhance the bustline. Look for twisted bandeau tops; ruffles or gathers at the bustline; bright colours, dramatic textures and patterns on the top half. Darker colours below.

■ *Narrow or sloping shoulders* – need broad, wide-set straps. Avoid halter necks at all costs, which will emphasise weak shoulders.

■ *Short legs* – high cut sides will lengthen and slim legs.

■ *Long legs* – low cut sides will shorten too-long legs.

■ *Broad shoulders* – look good in halter necks. Avoid wide-set straps if your shoulders are very broad as they will add to the problem.

TEN 'MUST HAVES' FOR BEACH STYLE

- *Sheer shirt* – the perfect cover-up for the beach which can also double as a lovely evening jacket paired with a silk camisole or bustier and evening trousers.
- *Pareos/sarongs* – long or short wraps to tie around the waist or hips over bikini or swimsuit. If you are petite, tie at the bustline for a long-line look. Tie at an angle if you are thick waisted.
- *Loose palazzo pants* – an alternative to the sarong for those who prefer trousers – especially flattering for the fuller figure teamed with the big sheer shirt.
- *Swim hats* – from Liz Taylor's svelte turbans to 'Carmen Miranda' inspired floral creations, these are now very much back in fashion to protect hair from sun and salt water.
- *Captain's hat* – crisp, white hats decorated with gold braid, stars or crests are a fun option for nautical costumes, which are in fashion *every* season.
- *Tortoise-shell sunglasses* – suit everyone with a tan, and come in all shapes and sizes to suit every personality. Team up with a silk scarf for 'Grace Kelly' chic.
- *Bandannas* – in polka dots, stripes or traditional cowboy patterns. Tie around the neck (to keep off the sun), around the head (to keep back the hair) or simply on your bag (for a stylish touch).
- *Wide-brimmed hat* – big straw hats, angular and crisp; floppy or turned-up, remain classic, timeless beach accessories – add a chiffon scarf to the hat for a Forties beach look.
- *Sneakers* – simple Fifties tie-styles or slip-on boat shoes are the daytime choice for practicality and comfort. (Plastic beach-shoes are *essential* for jelly-fish phobics!)
- *Large tote bag* – don't spoil it all with a plastic carrier bag – carry everything in style in a large, straw-decorated bag or plastic-lined canvas bag.

'Buying swimwear is a nightmare. I'm sure the mirrors are distorted.'

Fay, age 30

CHAPTER FOUR

LITTLE OR LARGE?

*I*F, IN THE previous chapter, you ticked petite/small boned or fuller figure/large boned as one of your proportion problems, take heart from the fact that you are actually a large per cent of the population. More than 47 percent of UK women are size 16 and over, and this figure is even greater in other countries. A similar proportion are petite (5'3" or under) and a large number of women actually come into both categories, being both small and fuller figured. *Six-foot, skinny models are 'genetic accidents'*; you are a real woman!

Your

For this reason, I have decided to dedicate a chapter to these most common figures in order to give advice in more detail. I know from my postbag that large and small women both have great difficulty in knowing how best to dress to make the most of their particular size.

> 'Petite reminds me of tiny, scuttling, creatures – not me at all.'
>
> *Carol, age 28*

PETITE FIGURE

For those of you who do not like the word 'petite', I apologise profusely! Although I fall into this category myself, and have bandied the term about for many years, I did not realise until I conducted my market research that some women (particularly *fuller figured*, short women), find it insulting and condescending. Apparently they associate it with 'bony, little creatures with tiny, scuttling feet'! I would very much like to find a suitable (non-insulting) replacement but have, so far, failed to do so – any

scale

suggestions will be gratefully accepted!

For those who are short and would like to look a few inches taller, simply follow these guidelines:

- *Keep it up.* The best piece of advice I have for those of you who are petite is to keep everything as high as possible – hairstyles, hemlines and bosoms included. Anything long and dangling will only give the effect of dragging you down into the ground when obviously the opposite effect is desired.

- *Keep people's attention focused upwards* with a shorter hairstyle (above the shoulder), high-placed brooches, snugly fitting earrings and knee-length skirts.

- *Keep a slim silhouette.* The problem arises, of course, when you want to follow fashion and wear long skirts, swinging necklaces and yards of chiffon scarf. In this situation you are best to keep your silhouette as slim as possible, avoiding very full, long skirts and particularly those that have any detail, such as a border pattern, at the hemline. Your hemline is the last horizontal line in your clothing before the floor and the wider it is, the shorter you will look.

- *Trouser trouble.* The horizontal line theory also applies to trousers – a very wide trouser leg, as seen in palazzo pants, will make it appear as though a very large weight has descended from the skies and squashed you into the ground! Leave the billowing, voluminous variety to the tall and leggy and stick to straight-leg or even tapered trousers to present a more flattering picture; only the narrowest of palazzos are good for petites. For this reason, ski-pants and leggings have been great news for shorter women for many years. If you want to follow fashion and wear a slightly wider trouser then give yourself that extra bit of height with a small platform or wedge shoe – definitely not a flat shoe.

- *Avoid ankle detail.* Still on the subject of trousers, avoid turn-ups which have the effect of shortening the length of the leg.

CASUAL

Narrow trousers add most height to a petite frame. For winter warmth find jackets and sweaters which are not too bulky, to avoid the 'Michelin Man' look. Keep patterns and accessories small to medium scale.

SMART

To gain valuable inches when petite, keep your silhouette as slim as possible – especially avoiding long, full skirts. Dressing all in one colour also helps, and it is best to keep the focus of attention high up with scarves, jewellery etc.

- *Monochromatic dressing.* Head-to-toe dressing all in one colour can be very attractive and slimming, and can also add the illusion of several inches to a less-than-average height. Baroness Thatcher, herself petite, became expert at this and as a consequence rose in stature and appeared much bigger to her adversaries than actually was the case! Navy hat, navy dress, navy stockings, navy shoes – this keeps the eye travelling quickly down the figure with no horizontal breaks. If you find this boring, at least tone your skirt, tights and shoes together and keep lighter, brighter and patterned fabrics to your top half.

- *Avoid colour 'blocks'.* Chopping yourself into many colour 'blocks' – red hat, white blouse, red belt, navy skirt, natural tights, red shoes – can look like a walking disaster on petite women, so beware! You really need to be tall to carry this off well.

- *Scale down.* Think medium to small for scale of accessories and patterns – medium scale if you are large boned or overweight as well as petite; small scale if you are small boned or underweight and petite. Oversized 'shoulder duster' earrings can easily be overpowering and draw attention to your lack of height, as can huge buttons, wide epaulettes and over-scaled patterns.

- *Lightweights and texture.* A small woman is much better in several layers of fine lambswool than one thick, chunky cable-knit sweater. Look for medium- to lightweight fabrics with little or no texture and an elegantly loose fit in all garments.

- *Foot note.* Avoid flat or very high heels. A medium heel will give you an extra inch or two whereas a very high stiletto draws attention downward and just looks like you're trying too hard! When you are petite, attempts to look taller should always be subtle.

FULLER FIGURE

I once ran a series of seminars for Weight Watchers on 'Stylish Dressing for Larger Ladies' and was horrified to be greeted with requests from all and sundry for information on how they should dress when they are thin! This I refused to do because I believe very strongly that women should make the most of themselves and maximise their potential whatever their age, shape or size. Here were groups of women who were willing to look plain, drab and boring until they reached their magical 'Target Weight', whereupon they would immediately undergo a dramatic metamorphosis and suddenly take an interest in fashion, cosmetics and accessories.

If you want to lose weight, it is much easier to do so when you look and feel good during the process. Many women fall by the wayside after a few months of dieting because they see no difference in the drab person in the mirror. If you wait to buy new clothes, try a new hairstyle, or change your cosmetics until the day you are slim, the chances are that you will never treat yourself to those important perks because that day may never arrive!

'When you're big you want to look just as fashionable as everyone else.'

Rosie, age 17

BIG CAN BE BEAUTIFUL

Not all large ladies want to lose weight, however, and nor should they if they are happy and confident with their size and it poses no medical problem. Role model for unashamed cream-cake eaters everywhere is British comedienne Dawn French, who, out of sheer frustration at the lack of fashionable, colourful clothes for those 'larger than life', has entered the world of retail fashion herself. Her fashion label, '1647', is dedicated to the 47 percent of British women who are size 16 and over – a market which in the past has been hugely neglected by the majority of the big name high-street retailers who now seem to be slowly awakening to this market.

So, whether you are overweight and wanting to part company with the odd spare tyre (or two); or, whether you are pleased to be plump; or if you are simply large-boned, which no amount of dieting will change, follow these very simple guidelines to dress your figure to best effect:

YOUR SCALE

EVENING

Fuller figures can look exceptionally glamorous in the right evening wear. Darker colours, matt fabrics, loose flowing tops and wide palazzo trousers are flattering and elegant. Keep accessories medium to large to complement your size.

- Always buy the right size – nothing is more guaranteed to make you look like a size 18 than buying a size 16 outfit that is too tight! Choose well-cut, roomy and comfortable clothes.
- Look for vertical and diagonal styling lines on garments – avoid as much horizontal detail as possible and small-scale patterns.
- Keep to fairly classic tailored lines, avoiding puff sleeves, frills and flounces. Solid, deep colours have a slimming effect. If you have light colouring, complement your face with light cosmetics, jewellery, scarves, etc. (See Chapter 6.)
- Make a bold statement and express your personality through bold accessories. Large earrings, necklaces, brooches and bags are essential – anything too small will make you look bigger by comparison. Large accessories can therefore make you look smaller.
- Open collars and lowish necklines will minimise a double chin or thick neck. Avoid chokers, very high necklines or tightly tied scarves.
- Wear substantial shoes, and tights/stockings that blend with your shoes and/or hemline. Dark, opaque tights will slenderise large legs.
- Make sure your hairstyle has width and volume so that your head looks scaled to your body and not like a pea on a drum! A short, close-to-the-head style or hair tied back can look out of proportion.
- Ample bosoms need a good bra with a broad band at the back to support the weight. Avoid seams, stripes, breast-pockets (particularly with buttons) and long necklaces which either 'collect' in the cleavage or hang over the precipice.
- Keep jackets/tops quite long (but not too long if you have short legs). Single-breasted jackets are more slimming. Wear shoulder pads if you have narrow and/or sloping shoulders to balance your hips.
- Straight-leg or gently tapered trousers look good. Avoid gathered ankles at all costs, as these make legs look like cocktail sausages! Wide palazzos can look good if you are not too short.

DAY

A fuller figure needs to stress the vertical as much as possible which this striped shirt does wonderfully. Open necklines reduce wide necks or double chins. Straight skirts with loose tunics and waistcoats worn on the outside are a comfortable daytime look.

YOUR SCALE

CHAPTER FIVE

CREATING ORDER FROM CHAOS

*P*ICTURE THE SCENE: A woman stands (in her underwear) in front of a bulging, open wardrobe; the rail sagging under the sheer weight of assorted garments; the hangers so jam-packed together that removing one requires the brute force of Arnold

Schwarzenegger; and the European shoe mountain is growing steadily upwards from the murky depths. Faced with this awesome sight, our woman sighs, 'I've

Your

nothing to wear . . .' Sounds familiar? This scenario is enacted daily in a million bedrooms around the world – usually to the audience of one bemused/irritated male who refuses to take the woman's plight seriously, seeing it as a mere ploy to buy yet another outfit. Next time this situation arises for you, strenuously resist the temptation to go out and buy yet another outfit, for this habit is, in fact, at the very heart of your problem.

When a woman says she 'has nothing to wear'; what she actually means is that she has worn the same old outfits over and over again for the past few weeks or months, is sick and tired of them, and cannot create a new outfit out of the myriad different colours, shapes and styles staring her in the face. Men, of course, don't understand this plight because they are brilliant at wardrobe planning – well, they have to be good at something . . .

Although they don't realise it, men have very organised, planned wardrobes – surprisingly enough, the majority of which is usually purchased by a woman! They work with neutral colours (grey, navy,

wardrobe

brown, etc) as the backbone of the wardrobe, with which they then mix lighter and brighter colours in different combinations.

The typical woman's wardrobe, however, consists of a wide array of different 'outfits' which have very little in common with each other – does the front cover of this book look like your wardrobe? This is largely because a woman buys for *occasions*, not for her wardrobe. She buys for an interview (sensible navy suit, blouse and shoes); for a wedding (pink silk dress with matching hat and bag); for Christmas (black puff-ball dress with sequins and 6″ stilettos); for holidays (orange sundress, cork wedge sandals, straw hat), etc.

She also buys on impulse ('the colour caught my eye, but it goes with nothing I have got . . .') and she buys in sales ('it was a bargain – it'll fit if I lose 7lbs . . .'). Nothing goes with anything else; everything must be worn in the way it was bought and cannot be mixed and matched with anything else to 'create' new outfits.

Every woman I have ever met wants to have a planned, organised wardrobe with most of the clothes being worn on a regular basis in different ways. Instead, research shows that she wears 20 percent of her wardrobe 80 percent of the time – the greatest crime being that the clothes that lie hanging in the wardrobe most of the time are usually the most expensive!

So, make the decision, once and for all, to organise and plan your wardrobe so that it caters easily and effortlessly for all your occasion and lifestyle needs. But where do you start on such a mammoth task? Follow me . . .

The first cut is the deepest; heap the contents of your wardrobe on to your bed and weed out the pieces which are outdated, ill-fitting, never worn or unflattering to your figure.

TEN-STEP PLAN TO THE
PERFECT WARDROBE

STEP 1 THE FIRST CUT IS THE DEEPEST

Go through your drawers, closets and cupboards and drag out everything that you haven't worn in the past eighteen months to two years. These will include items which:

- Are old fashioned/outdated (they never come back into fashion exactly the same)
- No longer fit (stop kidding yourself you'll slim into them)
- Were shopping mistakes/unwanted presents (your mother won't know)
- Don't suit your current lifestyle/desired image (ie your old student attire)
- Arc not flattering to your shape or proportions (see previous chapters)

Resolve to keep only clothing that makes the most of your good points and draws attention away from your not-so-good points. If you are thick waisted, don't keep very fitted garments or big belts; if you have good legs, keep the shorter skirts; if you have big, wide shoulders, remove shoulder padded garments, etc.

STEP 2 UNCLUTTER YOUR LIFE

If you are really serious about making a fresh start, get rid of all the above items to jumble sales or 'nearly new' shops. If this is too scary, pack the clothes away under a bed, in the spare room, on top of a wardrobe, and see how often you go to them over the next year. The chances are you never will, so get rid of them then. This will be a lot easier when you haven't clapped eyes on them for twelve months or more!

STEP 3 ASSESS THE REMAINS

What's left may look a little pathetic and meagre but at least there will be space in the wardrobe to hang your essential new purchases proudly. The contents of your wardrobe should now consist of all the items which are current and fashionable; fit you well; suit your lifestyle; and flatter your figure and face.

STEP 4 HANG IT ALL

Now reorganise the hanging style of your wardrobe. Never place a complete outfit on a hanger in the exact same way as you bought it or this is the only way you will ever appear in it. You will then get less wear out of it, and ultimately grow tired of it. Instead, hang your clothes in groups defined by *type* of garment, ie all jackets together, skirts together, trousers together, shirts together, etc. If you choose a different jacket, bottom and top each morning, you'll soon be amazed to find combinations of outfits you didn't realise you had!

STEP 5 KEEP A LIFESTYLE DIARY

As you will need to fill in the gaps in your wardrobe, it is essential to know which key pieces are missing. The best way to discover this is by keeping a Lifestyle Diary for at least a month. Put the following headings on several sheets of paper (stick them inside your wardrobe door) and fill them in religiously each time you get changed:

Date	Event/occasion	What I wore	What I wish I'd worn

The end column (What I wish I'd worn) is very revealing, as it pinpoints the gaps in your wardrobe and serves as a shopping list for your future purchases. Don't forget to include jewellery, shoes, bags, scarves, etc on your lists; if you are lacking in these items they make good birthday/anniversary suggestions for the coming year so display the list prominently!

STEP 6 CREATE A TIMELESS 'CORE'

The seasonless wardrobe has definitely arrived. Gone are the days of packing away your heavy tweeds, corduroys and winter woollies to the spare wardrobe for a six-month sabbatical where they hang festooned with moth-balls while your 'summer' wardrobe has its chance to see the light of day.

With our centrally heated and air-conditioned environments at home, work and even in the car, we are now living with less extremes of temperature. Couple this with the fact that women now lead more demanding and busy lifestyles which leave them with little time or inclination to perform the wardrobe-changeover routine twice yearly. The moth-ball business has not been a good one to invest in over the past decade.

Seasonless dressing is nothing new – to men, that is, who have never understood a woman's need to have two completely separate wardrobes. Take a leaf from your man's book and realise the importance of a wardrobe based around a backbone of lightweight suits, jackets and trousers which you layer up or down with sweaters, waistcoats, cardigans and coats as the changes in weather dictate. These items form the *core* of your wardrobe.

Choice of fabric is everything in achieving a totally flexible core wardrobe. Medium weight is best to take you from one end of the year to the other, and fabrics which are crease resistant and hang well are a must for busy, working women – particularly those who travel frequently. Look for rayon, crêpe, wool, linen and cotton blends, and lightweight flannel, gaberdine and denim. It is always worth spending to your limit on important core items which will be the real workhorses of your wardrobe. Beautiful tailoring, classic styling and attention to detail (quality buttons, for example) will

'I'm a shoe addict. Can't help it. Can't say no.'

Susan, age 25

make them clothes you'll just love to wear and wear. Colour is now irrelevant to seasons and is much more dictated by women's personal preference, mood or lifestyle. You can just as easily wear black for summer in the Nineties fashion climate, as you can wear sugar-almond pastels in the winter.

For your core items, however, I would recommend building a good selection of pieces in neutral colours – navy, brown, taupe, grey, camel – which mix and match effortlessly with all other lighter and brighter shades which you probably already have in your wardrobe.

Make sure your wardrobe has the following core classics which never date and suit all ages, lifestyles, personalities and colourings. Just be sure to select the best styles to complement your figure:

CLASSIC

A classic suit in a neutral shade in a real 'must-have' for every wardrobe. Don't always wear it as you bought it – here, a black suit jacket looks chic teamed with a polo neck sweater and tartan skirt.

- *Little black dress.* Yes, it's a cliché but every wardrobe needs one. Ideal for 'black-tie' functions when your man is in his tuxedo. Black, as everyone knows, is *the* most slimming of colours as long as the fabric is matt. Personalise it with your favourite choice of accessories, shoes and make-up for the impact you desire!

- *Navy blazer.* For effortless, continental chic, a good blazer cannot be beaten. For a casual look, wear it with jeans and T-shirt; on semi-casual days team it with a sweater and classic trousers; and with a silk blouse and tailored skirt it can take you to the smartest of occasions. A blazer can even be invaluable for evenings – with elegant palazzo pants, a camisole top and gold jewellery to echo the blazer buttons.

- *White or ivory shirt.* In my experience, pure white is the most difficult colour to wear next to the face for many people, not black. If your colouring is very deep or bright (see next chapter) a pure white silk or satin blouse can look stunning but, for lighter or more muted colour patterns, ivory or oyster white will be kinder to the complexion. Warm-toned, freckled skins, particularly with red hair, will always look best with cream. Keep the shirt as simple in design as possible so that it could even be worn with jeans on casual

BLACK

An indispensable
cliché – the little
black dress. Choose
one in the best
shape for your
figure in a simple
fabric which can be
accessorized for
days or evening.

NEUTRALS

Neutrals are the backbone of the
wardrobe as they mix with all
colours. Use them for expensive
items such as coats, hats, suits
and leather accessories.

DENIM

Denim never goes out of fashion.
Select a medium-weight dress to
suit your shape and wear it alone
with strappy sandals in summer,
or with a shirt or thin sweater,
socks and boots in winter.

KNITWEAR

Medium-weight knitwear in neutral colours works well layered for winter warmth or singly as a light jacket for summer evening. Cotton knits are most versatile as they remain itch-free in summer and work well with heavy fabrics in winter.

occasions. Some stunning jewellery will transform it for parties.

■ *Cotton knitwear.* Much more versatile than chunky, woollen knitwear as it will keep you snug and warm in the winter, layered with shirts, blouses and jackets, while keeping your skin cool and itch-free in the summer. A really good investment would be a sweater-set comprising a sleeveless or short-sleeved sweater with matching cardigan. In the hot summer months wear the sweater alone with shorts or skirt, keeping the cardigan at hand to slip on for cooler evenings. In the winter, wear the sweater as a layering piece under a shirt with the cardigan on top teamed with jacket and trousers.

■ *Co-ordinated suit.* If you come across a medium-weight, neutral-coloured suit in a rayon blend comprising several pieces – jacket, skirt, trousers, waistcoat, shorts – buy the entire ensemble for effortless, seasonless combinations. Worn with shirts, ties, sweaters, knitted tank-tops, men's scarves, top coats, hats and gloves – the winter permutations are endless. In summer, or for winter social evenings, the jacket and skirt, or waistcoat and trousers are elegant by themselves with strappy shoes and dainty bags.

■ *Sleeveless dress.* My fabric recommendation for a timeless, seasonless, all-purpose dress would be lightweight denim. Sleeveless and button-fronted is most versatile but choose a straighter or more fitted style dependent on your body shape. In winter, team it with a sweater, tights and boots, while in summer, its only essential accessories are flat leather sandals and tanned legs glimpsed through the long unbuttoned skirt. For cooler, summer days, a cotton T-shirt can be layered beneath or a crisp white shirt knotted on top.

■ *Raincoat.* Make sure it's roomy enough to take a jacket and sweater underneath in the winter but light enough in weight not to be too stifling in summer. For these reasons, an elegant, swing-style of raincoat will give ample coverage for layered clothing in winter, while hanging loose over a simple slip dress on summer evenings. Edge-to-edge, buttonless styles can be ideal for summer – but make sure a detachable belt is available to wrap up warm against chill, winter winds. A traditional 'Burberry'-style trench coat is ideal for the straighter or angular figure.

STEP 7 START TO BUILD CAPSULES

As well as the timeless core items, successful wardrobes also contain several 'capsules', ie garments which co-ordinate together to create dozens of different outfits. Start with a basic capsule based around three colours:

- 2 suits that mix and match (one neutral and one coloured)
- 3 tops (blouses, shirts, T-shirts)
- 1 two-piece dress (matching skirt and top)
- 1 pair of classic trousers (neutral to match suit)
- 1 long, structured cardigan (to double as jacket)
- 1 sweater

The twelve different garments above can be mixed and matched to create over seventy outfits which can be dressed up or down for different occasions with a variety of accessories – belts, jewellery, scarves, hats, etc. If you have any of the above pieces, use them as the basis of your new plan and put the rest on your shopping list. Although you may have halved the contents of your wardrobe, a few well-chosen additions can increase its potential tenfold!

STEP 8 SHOP AT THE BEGINNING OF EACH SEASON

When the autumn/winter fashions are coming into the high street the sun may still be shining on your patio (you may even have not been away for your summer break yet!), but this is by far the best time to start planning your winter wardrobe. Depressing as it may be to contemplate spending several hours in a stuffy changing room, slowly covering your newly acquired tan with winter layers, remember that it is always the early fashion bird that catches the best buys. Spring/summer clothes similarly need to be bought before winter is over.

RAINCOAT

Top it all with a quality raincoat to take you to any occasion. Short and swingy for the petite and/or curvy figure; long, trench coat style for the tall and/or straighter figure.

A CAPSULE FOR YOUR WORKING LIFE

EASY PIECES TO MIX 'N' MATCH

Most retailers now design 'capsule' ranges of co-ordinating separates – jackets, skirts, trousers, sweaters, cardigans and waistcoats – which all mix and match together to make a myriad different outfits. This is a complete godsend for busy women (or women who just *hate* shopping) as all the essentials of the season can be bought in one fell swoop under one roof. Thankfully, gone are all the times that demanded several back-breaking shopping sprees per season, visiting dozens of different shops in the vain attempt to match one navy to another. Today, all the hard work is done for you; so take my advice and always shop at the beginning of the season when stocks are high. Nothing is more frustrating than returning to a store shortly after you've purchased a suit to buy the matching trousers and waistcoat, to find that only size 8s remain . . .

Here are two simple capsule wardrobes with versatile pieces in each. The first is based around a 'city' or working lifestyle; the second around a 'country' or more leisurely existence. The garments shown can be mixed and matched to create dozens of different outfits. It is quite easy to put together a week's wardrobe from just eight easy pieces without wearing the same outfit twice.

'I'd love a planned, organised wardrobe – but where do you start?'

Claire, age 35

WARDROBE A: 'CITY'/WORKING

eg grey, red, white

1 Jacket – collarless is most versatile
2 Short skirt – curved or straight
3 Trousers – classic leg
4 Long skirt – straight, wrap-over, or flared
5 Waistcoat
6 Blouse – white
7 Blouse – colour
8 Cardigan
9 Shirt – striped
10 Dress
11 Extra jacket

WARDROBE B: 'COUNTRY'/LEISURE

eg brown, green, spice

1 Jacket, eg Norfolk, belted
2 Trousers – tweed, flecked
3 Jodhpurs – plain
4 Skirt – short or long
5 Waistcoat – suede, sheepskin, patchwork, etc
6 Shirt – plain, eg chambray
7 Shirt – patterned, eg tattersall check
8 Sweater – cable-knit
9 Shirt – collarless
10 Extra jacket
11 Jeans

THE PERFECT HOLIDAY CAPSULE

One of the most frequently received letters in my postbag is the one asking for advice on what to take on holiday. If you are one of those women who takes almost the entire contents of her wardrobe on holiday (including ten pairs of shoes!) and still doesn't have the right outfits when you get there, simply study the capsule below which all fits into one small case – and you won't need the whole family to sit on the lid to lock it!

TWELVE EASY PIECES
FOR TWO WEEKS IN THE SUN

1 Trouser suit
   - Neutral colour to mix 'n' match with everything
   - Linen blend to prevent creasing when travelling
   - Long-line jacket and straight trousers suit all shapes

2 Skirt suit
   - Colour and fabric that will mix with trouser suit
   - Short skirt or long split skirt to show tanned legs
   - Collarless jacket most versatile for holidays

3 Shorts
   - Chosen to blend with both suit jackets
   - Knee-length most slimming and also good for evenings
   - Roll them and put in your hand luggage for a quick change at the airport!

A CAPSULE FOR YOUR LEISURE LIFE

EASY PIECES TO MIX 'N' MATCH

4 Tops
- T-shirts or bodies in light or bright colours (dependent on your colouring and personal tastes)
- Camisole or blouse in 'your' white for evenings (See Chapter 6)
- Waistcoat – to wear alone on hot days or to layer on cooler days or evenings

5 Two-piece dress
- In a pattern that mixes with both suits
- Button-front shirt doubles as a light jacket
- Knot the blouse under bust and wear with shorts/trousers

6 Cotton-knit
- Baggy sweater for casual daytime look
- Cardigan-style doubles as a jacket
- Neutral colour most versatile

7 Sarong skirt
- With T-shirt/blouse for day
- With camisole, jewellery, etc for evening
- As beach cover-up over swimwear

8 Straight, slip-dress – plain
- With flat shoes, scarf, etc for day
- With heels, jewellery for evening
- With trousers as tunic for day or evening

9 Button-front dress (patterned)
- Wear alone
- Layer over trousers, shorts, beachwear, etc
- Long side slits allow front to be tied as blouse

10 Palazzos
- With body and jacket
- With knotted white blouse
- With camisole and jewellery

11 Pareo/square wrap (exotic colours)
- As beach cover-up (over hips or tie over bust as dress)
- Drape over simple slip dress as scarf for evening
- Can be tied around neck and waist to make halter top

12 Sun hats
- Large brimmed straw (pack at bottom of case with crown stuffed with socks/undies)
- Panama that rolls into tube for travelling
- Canvas hat that folds easily into hand luggage

ACCESSORIES

1 Shoes (neutral colour)
- Leather thong flat sandals
- Canvas espadrilles
- Sandals for evenings

2 Bags
- Large leather tote bag for travelling
- Big straw beach bag
- Small clutch or shoulder bag for evenings

3 Scarves
- Bandanna for beach wear
- Long chiffon or silk for evenings
- Cotton or linen for daywear

4 Jewellery
- Casual beads, bangles and earrings
- Muted, brushed gold to complement tan
- Pearls or crystal for evenings

A CAPSULE FOR YOUR PERFECT HOLIDAY

EASY PIECES TO MIX 'N' MATCH

Cost = Price × Times Worn, choose separates for evening wear, such as this overshirt and black skirt, both of which have life after the party's over as daytime wear.

STEP 9 RESIST 'LIMITED LIFE' OUTFITS FOR SPECIAL OCCASIONS

If the real cost of an item is its price multiplied by the amount of times you wear it, then logic tells us that items which constitute the biggest waste of money in our wardrobe are those frothy party frocks which cost the earth, make an appearance once or twice and are then consigned to the far recesses of the wardrobe gathering dust and guilt. The problem with little numbers such as these is that they either date very quickly (hands up, who's still got a stretch velvet tube dress with a taffeta puff-ball skirt . . .?) or, even if your dress has survived the fickleness of the past year's fashion, you can't possibly wear it again to this year's round of business and social functions because everyone (oh, the shame of it!) will recognise it immediately.

One solution to this problem is to spend the intervening months between each Christmas searching for a different job and completely new circle of friends. (Family, unfortunately, are more difficult to dispense with, but they're more understanding about seeing you in the same dress twice anyway.) Alternatively, you could be sensible and experiment with a spot of 'Investment Buying', which has nothing to do with gilt-edged bonds and *everything* to do with guilt-free party outfits.

The secret of successful investment buys is that they have a life beyond the occasion for which they were purchased. That pink silk dress, with matching pink hat, shoes and handbag bought for cousin Brenda's wedding is a waste of money – unless, of course, money is no object! Much wiser (and fashionable) is to buy a simple, chic suit which can be 'dressed-up' with accessories for the wedding, but then worn countless other times throughout the year: for work (with smart shirts); for leisure (with T-shirts); for evenings (with camisole, lace bustier), etc.

Similarly for parties, I would recommend that you buy elegant separates – black skirts or trousers with fancy tops, jackets, tunics or waistcoats – which will still have plenty of use in your wardrobe after the party's over.

STEP 10 KNOW THE 'MUST HAVES' EACH SEASON

The secret of keeping your wardrobe looking up to date and fashionable is to add key accessories and small garments to your basic 'core' and 'capsules'. You do not need to buy completely new 'outfits' each season, but by simply adding the right, inexpensive accessories and small fashion pieces you can create the current looks on even the smallest budget.

Familiarise yourself with the different themes each season and the 'must have' items which will update your wardrobe immediately. (See page 160 for details of how to obtain the Fashion Portfolio which provides all this information twice yearly.) A simple, classic suit can be transformed with the right know-how into the perfect outfit for a country weekend, a shopping trip with friends, a board-room presentation, or a night on the town.

WARDROBE PLANNING SUMMARY

- Stop buying only for occasions and on impulse
- Weed your wardrobe – get rid of anything not worn in the past two years!
- Start buying for your wardrobe, to make it flexible
- Spend most money on items you'll wear most often (core classics)
- Never buy something unless it goes with three other items (capsule pieces)
- Consider your present lifestyle and clothing needs – make sure the *balance* of your wardrobe reflects this
- Invest in good accessories to dress outfits up or down
- Buy for who you are now – not for a 'slimmer' you
- Understand your best shapes and styles for successful mixing
- Know the 'must haves' each season

Or choose a classically-styled black dress, such as this empire-line style, which will not date dramatically and quickly go out of fashion. Hands up who's got a taffeta puff-ball dress at home?

CHAPTER SIX

COLOUR ANALYSIS

*S*INCE THE SEVENTIES, there have been many systems devised by different colour-analysis companies to determine an individual's best colours. Although this practice may have been beneficial, in that it has made us all more aware of colour, most of the systems used have been very limiting, usually based on a 'seasonal' concept which forces us to choose all warm or all cool colours. Worst of all is the suggestion that we have to stay in these colours forever, which can be terminally boring.

Your

> '*I wouldn't want to be "packaged-up" by a colour consultant.*'
>
> *Mavis, age 23*

Everybody (myself included, as you will know from my introduction) who has had 'their colours done' by a colour analyst will recognise the frustrations and fears inherent in such a system: What if I don't *like* the colours recommended for me? What about the *expense* if I don't have any of the right colours in my current wardrobe? What if the colours suggested are not *in fashion* at the moment? What if my *personality* requires a totally different set of colours?

Being restricted to one wallet of colours for evermore can turn shopping into a nightmare if you are trudging the streets searching for 'winter' fuchsia pink, pillarbox red and emerald green, when the rest of the fashionable world is swathed in shades of olive, beige and brown. And, to be perfectly blunt, after a year or two you may begin to look and feel predictable, boring and in desperate need of a dramatic change.

If you have 'had your colours done' by one of the more rigid

colouring

systems and it has improved your looks and confidence; you happen to like all the colours; they are easy to find; and they suit your personality – then, by all means stick to them and continue to enjoy the discipline it has brought to your life and wardrobe. I would suggest, however, that you don't become *too* dependent on your swatch wallet as you are probably missing out on lots of delicious colours which would suit you equally well. It always depresses me to see a woman in a shop holding clothing to her swatch wallet for an *exact* match or refusing to look at a gorgeous outfit suggested by an assistant because the colour is not *exactly* the same as in her swatch wallet.

If you have a swatch wallet already, remember three things:

Hair and eyes are just as important as skin tone to find your best colours.

- **A swatch is a signpost not a prison** – it is merely showing the *kinds* of colours that suit you, not the only colours in the world for you.
- **Fabric swatches vary in dye density**. Fuchsia pink in one 'winter' swatch and fuchsia pink in another 'winter' swatch can vary in depth or brightness, depending on which dye-batch they came from. Trying to match your swatch piece to an article of clothing is therefore a pointless exercise, as it is 'pot luck' as to which dye-lot yours came from! For this reason, I only recommend printed swatch cards, which are then viewed much more as a 'rough' guide and they also don't tempt people to try and match them to clothing colours, because they are not made of fabric.
- **A swatch is no substitute for a brain!** If you need to carry a swatch wallet around with you, you don't really understand your colouring. I believe swatches should not be expensive, because you only need to look at them a couple of times; once you know their message, you can throw them away! You should be able to apply the 'message' of your swatch to each different fashion season and make colour selections accordingly.

HAIR AND EYES
ARE AS IMPORTANT AS SKIN

Sometimes colour analysts will begin draping you in fabrics to see if you have a warm or cool undertone. Some even cover the hair with a turban and ask you to close your eyes in the belief that your clothing colours should be determined by your skin tone alone. As we don't walk around in real life with a bag on our heads and our eyes shut, this seems quite a ridiculous practice to me! Sometimes you can also be asked to put your hand onto a piece of gold (warm) or silver (cool) fabric to help the analysis; this is also crazy, as the skin on your hands can differ enormously from the skin on your face – your hands do the washing-up for instance!

Sometimes the hair or eyes can be *the* most striking aspect of a person's colouring – far more important than warm or cool skin. In my opinion, when selecting 'best' colours for an individual, you have to take into account the total picture – hair, eyes and skin – which is how the person is viewed in reality. You also have to analyse the way she has decided to present herself to the world, which is very much tied up with her personality. If she has decided to be blonde or a redhead, or has even dyed her hair plum and taken to wearing bright green contact lenses – those are the characteristics on which you should make any recommendations, not on the fact that she has a warm complexion or *naturally* mousey hair and grey eyes!

MOST PEOPLE CAN
WEAR WARM AND COOL COLOURS

When you look at *the total picture* of your colouring you will find that 90 percent of people are a complete mixture of warm and cool elements and can therefore wear colours from either group depending on their personal preference, mood or fashion. Only 10 percent of people have so much warmth in their colouring (caused by the pigment carotene); or so much coolness (caused by the blue-brown pigment melanin) that they really do look better sticking to all-warm or all-cool colours. But even these people can learn how to wear any colour they want to, simply by keeping their best colours

'My wardrobe's a complete mix of colours – I definitely need help.'

Judy, age 28

next to the face – in other words, they can learn to mix warm and cool colours together.

Some colour analysts throw up their arms in horror when I say you can mix warm and cool colours – always telling me that this never happens in nature and is therefore not harmonious. It is presumptuous to suppose that everyone *wants* to look harmonious – some extrovert personalities simply don't want to. Also, it is completely wrong to say that nature does not mix warm and cool together – a toucan is black (cool) and orange (warm); a sunset is fuchsia (cool) and orange (warm); and there is no nicer sight than a (warm) yellow sun in a (cool) blue sky.

UNIVERSAL COLOURS

Some colours, in fact, cannot be classed as either warm or cool and are therefore very 'safe' and can be worn equally well by everyone. For this reason they are often known as *universal* colours and comprise the following:

- Watermelon red (a light, pinky shade of red)
- Turquoise (a yellowy shade of blue)
- Violet (a yellowy shade of purple)
- Teal (a cross between blue and green – like a duck's neck)
- Coral pink (a yellowy shade of pink)
- Maize (a light, greyish shade of yellow)
- Ivory (a creamy shade of white)

Whether you are dark, fair or sallow skinned; brown, blue or green eyed; jet black, brown, red, blonde or mousey haired – the above universal colours will suit you perfectly.

If you are getting married in the near future, and have an assortment of different colour patterns in your choice of bridesmaids, select their dresses from the universal list and you can't go far wrong!

THE
UNIVERSAL
COLOURS
which suit every colouring.

NEUTRAL COLOURS

These are the most *useful* colours to have in your wardrobe and no woman can afford to be without them. Although they may seem boring on their own, they mix and match with *all* other colours and are essential for major items such as suits, trousers, coats, etc.

■ Black ■ Brown ■ Navy ■ Grey ■ Taupe ■ Camel ■ Beige

Depending on your colouring, you may look good in some of these neutrals on their own; others you may need to team up with another colour next to the face to make them work better for you. The next section will show you exactly how to do that.

FINDING YOUR COLOUR DIRECTION

Study the descriptions of the most common colour patterns on the following pages and find the one which is closest to how you look *at present* – remember, this may not be how nature intended you to look, but how you *like* to look. My advice will then give you not only your most harmonious colours, but how to wear *any* colour you happen to like. The direction of your colouring may change if you colour your hair, deepen your skin tone (eg false tan) or wear coloured contact lenses, so always refer back to this chapter if you decide to make any dramatic changes to your appearance.

Also, as you age, your colouring can alter quite significantly – you could be blonde in your twenties, dark in your thirties and forties, and then grey in your fifties and beyond. Don't assume therefore, that the advice you read today will hold true forever.

Because your colouring can change throughout your life (with or without help!) I prefer to talk about 'Colour Directions' rather than strict colour categories or pigeon-holes. Know and understand your current Colour Direction, but always bear in mind that you can decide to change direction at any time if age, boredom, fashion or a change of lifestyle (eg divorce!) gives you cause.

THE
NEUTRAL
COLOURS
every wardrobe needs a good selection.

Above: Light glasses with deep colouring become an obvious feature on the face.

Top: Deep colouring has the strength to take strong cosmetic shades and intense clothing colours next to the face – even a burgundy hair colour!

DEEP DIRECTION

eg Cher, Paloma Picasso, Oprah Winfrey

This colour pattern is the most common throughout the world, particularly in southern climes, and is often described as strong, powerful or dark. If you have been made a 'season', it is probably a 'winter' or an 'autumn' – although your colouring may be a mixture of warm and cool elements.

Hair colours: Black, dark to mid-brown, chestnut (not red).
Eye colours: Dark brown, deep hazel, olive green, navy blue.
Skin tone: Medium to dark (often tans easily).
Your best neutral colours: Black, charcoal grey, dark brown, deep navy. These are also good colours for leather accessories.
How to wear black: on its own looks great!
Your best version of white: Pure white.
Examples of harmonious colours: Deep purple, forest green, burgundy, royal blue.
In a fashion season: Any deep, strong, intense colours will suit you well.
Your opposite colours: Light, pale, pastel shades, eg powder pink, baby blue, beige, cream, lemon. Wearing these alone, particularly close to the face, can be difficult unless you have great style and confidence in your looks, and/or have an extrovert personality! If you fear wearing them alone, simply team them with a deeper, stronger, intense colour next to the face (eg scarf, blouse or necklace). If you choose glasses frames in these lighter shades, remember that they will stand out from your face and be obvious.
Change of hair colour:

- if you go grey (more than 50 percent) you will be heading in the Cool Direction
- if you go red (more than 50 percent) you will be heading in the Warm Direction
- if you go blonde (more than 50 percent) you will be heading in the Muted Direction

LIGHT DIRECTION

eg Princess Diana, Kylie Minogue, Goldie Hawn

This colour pattern is very common in western countries, particularly Scandinavia, and is often described as fair, delicate or soft. If you have been made a 'season', it is possibly a 'summer' or 'spring' – although your colouring may well be a mixture of warm and cool elements.

Hair colour: Golden blonde, ash blonde, light brown/mousey, yellow grey.
Eye colour: Blue, green, grey, blue/grey, green/grey.
Skin tone: Medium to light (often does not tan easily).
Your best neutral colours: Dove grey, light brown, taupe, beige, light navy. These are also good colours for leather accessories.
How to wear black: with a lighter colour or light jewellery.
Your best version of white: Ivory. Pure white is a *deep* colour and can look good with a light colouring when you have a tan.
Examples of harmonious colours: Powder pink, denim blue, mint green, lavender.
In a fashion season: Any light, delicate, soft colours will suit you well.
Your opposite colours are deep, strong, dark ones, eg burgundy, aubergine, black, bottle green, deep purple. Wearing these alone, particularly very close to the face, can be difficult unless you have great style and confidence in your looks, and/or have an extrovert personality! If you fear wearing them alone, simply team them with a lighter, softer, delicate colour next to the face (eg scarf, blouse or necklace). If you choose glasses frames in these darker shades, remember that they will stand out from your face and be obvious.
Change of hair colour:

- if you go steely grey (more than 50 percent) you will be heading in the Cool Direction
- if you go darker (more than 50 percent) you will be heading in the Bright Direction
- if you go red/copper (more than 50 percent) you will be heading in the Warm Direction.

Above: Deep, strong colours can be used with light colouring for a bold, dramatic look.

Top: Light colouring looks harmonious with softer cosmetics and clothing colours.

BRIGHT DIRECTION

eg Liz Taylor, Joan Collins, Princess Caroline

This colour pattern, which is characterised by a great contrast between hair, skin and eyes, is very Celtic in origin, and is often described as sharp, vivid or clear. If you have been made a 'season', it is probably a 'winter' or 'spring', although your colouring may well be a mixture of warm and cool elements.

Hair colour: Black, medium to dark brown, chestnut. Hair can be grey or blonde if eyebrows are *very dark*.
Eye colour: Bright blue, green, turquoise, bright hazel, violet.
Skin tone: Light to medium (may tan or burn).
Your best neutral colours: Black, bright navy, charcoal grey, medium brown. These are also good colours for leather accessories.
How to wear black: with a bright colour or bright, shiny jewellery.
Your best version of white: With a tan – pure white. Pale skinned – off white.
Examples of harmonious colours: Fuchsia pink, emerald green, poppy red, peacock blue.
In a fashion season: Any bright, clear, vivid, sharp colours will suit you well.
Your opposite colours are soft, dusky, muted shades, eg beige, sage green, dusky rose, mustard, powder blue. Wearing these alone, particularly very close to the face, can be difficult unless you have great style and confidence in your looks, and/or have an extrovert personality! If you fear wearing them alone, simply team them with a brighter, clearer or more vivid colour next to the face (eg scarf, blouse or necklace). If you choose glasses frames in these muted shades, remember that they will stand out from your face.
Change of hair colour:

- if you go steely grey (more than 50 percent) you will be heading in a Cool Direction
- if you go blonde/yellow grey (more than 50 percent) you will be heading in a Light Direction
- if you go red/copper (more than 50 percent) you will be heading in a Warm Direction

Above: When wearing your opposite colour direction – such as this muted lipstick – make sure your hairstyle is stylish and perfect for your face and features to avoid looking drab.

Top: Bright colouring can take vivid colours, strong contrast and shiny jewellery easily – with a surprisingly sophisticated look.

MUTED DIRECTION

eg Cindy Crawford, Hannah Gordon, Jemima Goldsmith

This colour pattern is quite unusual and does not occur very frequently in natural colour patterns. It is characterised by light hair with darker eyes and is often described as soft, rich or blended. If you have been made a 'season', it is probably a 'summer' or 'autumn', although your colouring may well be a mixture of warm and cool elements.

Hair colour: Blonde, light brown/mousey, yellow grey.
Eye colour: Brown, hazel, olive green, greeny/grey.
Skin tone: Medium to deep (may tan or burn).
Your best neutral colours: Soft grey, greyed navy, taupe, camel. These are also good colours for leather accessories.
How to wear black: with a muted colour or brushed, matt gold jewellery near the face.
Your best version of white: Oyster.
Examples of harmonious colours: Dusty rose, sage green, air force blue, aubergine.
In a fashion season: Any muted, soft, rich, blended colours will suit you well.
Your opposite colours are sharp, bright, clear colours, eg fuchsia pink, pure white, emerald green, scarlet. Wearing these alone, particularly very close to the face, can be difficult unless you have great style and confidence in your looks, and/or have an extrovert personality! If you fear wearing them alone, simply team them with softer, richer, more blended colour next to the face (eg scarf, blouse or necklace). If you choose glasses frames in these brighter shades, remember they will stand out from your face and be obvious.
Change of hair colour:

- if you go dark (more than 50 percent) you will be heading in a Deep Direction
- if you go steely grey (more than 50 percent) you will be heading in a Cool Direction
- if you go red/copper (more than 50 percent) you will be heading in a Warm Direction

Above: If your personality needs brighter colours, make sure the style and fit of your outfit is perfect to carry off what could be an overpowering look.

Top: Muted colouring is both soft and strong – harmonious ones are not too bright.

Above: Cooler colours, such as this fuchsia pink, can be worn if you feel confident with your face and body.

Top: Warm colouring looks perfect in earthy shades with gold or tortoiseshell glasses.

WARM DIRECTION

eg Duchess of York (Fergie), Rula Lenska, Nicole Kidman

This golden, burnished colour pattern is often associated with northern countries – particularly Scotland – and is characterised by an abundance of the pigment carotene in hair, eyes and often on the skin as freckles. If you have been made a 'season', it is probably a 'spring' or 'autumn' and you probably have little evidence of cool elements in your colouring (unless you have dyed your hair red).

Hair colour: Red, auburn, copper, ginger.
Eye colour: Brown, hazel, bright blue/turquoise, green.
Skin tone: Golden or very pale (often burns easily and freckles).
Your best neutral colours: Brown, camel, tan, marine navy, rust, terracotta. These are also good colours for leather accessories.
How to wear black: with a warm colour or gold jewellery.
Your best version of white: Cream.
Examples of harmonious colours: Tomato red, turquoise, apple green, peach, coral.
In a fashion season: Any warm, golden, fiery or burnished colours will suit you well.
Your opposite colours are cool, icy or bluey colours, eg white, ice-blue, pale pink, fuchsia, raspberry. Wearing these alone, particularly very close to the face, can be difficult unless you have great style and confidence in your looks, and/or have an extrovert personality! If you fear wearing them alone, simply team them with warmer, golden or more fiery colours next to the face (eg scarf, blouse or necklace). If you choose glasses frames in these cool shades, remember that they will stand out of your face and be obvious.
Change of hair colour:
- if you go dark (more than 50 percent) and have brown/hazel eyes you will be heading in the Deep Direction
- if you go dark (more than 50 percent) and have blue/turquoise/green eyes you will be heading in the Bright Direction
- if you go blonde (more than 50 percent) and have brown/hazel eyes you will be heading in the Muted Direction
- if you go blonde (more than 50 percent) and have blue/turquoise/green eyes you will be heading in the Light Direction

COOL DIRECTION

eg Queen Elizabeth, Germaine Greer, Barbara Bush

This silvery, ashy colour pattern is often associated with older women who have gone grey – although you can, of course, go grey at quite a young age, and some brown/mousey-haired colour patterns have so little warmth in their colouring that they also fall mostly in the Cool Direction. If you have been made a 'season', it is probably a 'summer' or 'winter'.

Hair colour: White, steely grey, ash/mousey brown.
Eye colour: Blue, blue/grey, grey, greyish brown.
Skin tone: Deep, rosy or ashy (very few freckles).
Your best neutral colours: Any grey, any navy, taupe, black (with dark eyes). These are also good colours for leather accessories.
How to wear black: looks good on its own if you have a deep complexion and dark eyes. Otherwise wear it with a cool colour or silver jewellery near the face.
Your best version of white: Pure white (if tanned) or soft white.
Examples of harmonious colours: Royal blue, cerise, bluey greens, icy lilac, blood red.
In a fashion season: Any cool, icy or bluey colours will suit you well.
Your opposite colours are warm, golden or yellowy colours, eg orange, lime green, egg yellow, tan. Wearing these alone, particularly very close to the face, can be difficult unless you have great style and confidence in your looks! If you fear wearing them alone, simply team them with cooler, clearer more bluey colours next to the face. If you choose glasses frames in these warmer shades, remember that they will stand out from your face.
Change of hair colour:

- if you go dark (more than 50 percent) and have brown eyes you will be heading in the Deep Direction
- if you go dark (more than 50 percent) and have light eyes you will be heading in the Bright Direction
- if you go blonde (more than 50 percent) and have dark eyes you will be heading in the Muted Direction
- if you go blonde (more than 50 percent) and have light eyes you will be heading in the Light Direction

Above: Cool colouring can look sharp and dynamic with a fashionable hairstyle and current clothes. Grey doesn't have to be ageing!

Top: Cool colouring shows no evidence of warmth and looks best with all traces of yellow removed from the hair, plus cooler cosmetic shades.

CHAPTER SEVEN

ANALYSING YOUR FACE

*I*N CHAPTER 1 we took a long hard look at your face to analyse its outline and features in order to work out your best hairstyle, glasses and necklines. We'll take another good look at it again now, without make-up and with your hair pushed back, to see how clever use of cosmetics can accentuate your positive features and minimise your negative ones.

'Buying make-up really cheers you up.'

Caroline, age 44

SKIN

The skin on your face is very delicate and should be protected as much as possible from exterior ele- *Your* ments – central heating, intense sun, cold weather, etc. What you take into your body affects your skin also – a poor diet, excess alcohol and cigarette smoke have adverse affects. Couple these with lack of exercise and a stressful life and you begin to see tell-tale signs on your face. Spots, broken veins, dry or oily patches and dark circles under the eyes are all warnings to change your diet, lifestyle or skincare regime. If you have any of these problems *regularly* (we all get the odd spot now and again!), don't use make-up to cover up the problem but visit a skin specialist for advice on how to achieve skin which is healthier and even in tone, colour and texture.

EYEBROWS

I find that eyebrows are the most neglected area of a woman's face and yet they are *so* vital to achieving fantastic make-up results. Eyebrows are very important as they frame the eye and, if properly outlined, can make eyes look bigger and more attractive. It is

cosmetics

therefore essential for eyebrows to be seen!

If your eyebrows are very fair or grey, use a taupe or light-brown eyebrow pencil – or even a brown eye-shadow with a very thin brush – to coat gently the hairs already there. If your eyebrows have disappeared completely – whether through age or because you plucked them all out and they didn't grow back! – pencil them in a pale shade using small feathery strokes rather than a thick, dark, heavy line.

If your eyebrows are very bushy and unruly, they can dominate your face and take the emphasis away from your eyes. It is wise to thin them into an elegant shape – but only ever pluck from underneath (to clear the orbital bone) and never start further out than the inner corner of the eye.

EYES

These are the most important feature of the face as it is where people's attention is focused during conversation – not the mouth. Making the most of your eyes is essential, particularly if, like me, you don't like another feature on your face such as your mouth, teeth, nose or chin! Look at your eyes carefully – are they big or small?, Close-set or wide-set?, Deep-set or prominent?, Straight or downward-turned? Clever use of eye-shadows, pencils and mascara can counteract any of these problems.

CHEEKS

Do your cheekbones stand out prominently or are they camouflaged by more rounded, fleshy cheeks? Congratulations if you answered 'yes' to the former as high, prominent cheekbones are always an asset – make sure your hairstyle shows them off to good advantage. If you need to suck your cheeks in very hard to make your cheekbones appear, take heart – the illusion of cheekbones can be created with blusher.

Hold a pencil against your face (as shown above) to find the best length for your eyebrows.

LIPS

Most women wear lipstick. It is the quickest and easiest of all cosmetics to apply – some women can even apply it in restaurants after a meal without a mirror! But put a little more thought into how best to apply your lipstick depending on the shape of your mouth. Is it small and rosebudish or wide and letter-boxish? Are your lips equal in proportion or is one fuller and one thinner? Is the shape sharp and clearly defined or kind of 'blurred' around the edges? Clever use of lipsticks and pencils works wonders for lips.

MAKE-UP TECHNIQUES

When I am called upon to do makeovers for TV, the make-up is always the last part of the transformation and, as we are always working to a tight schedule, I am invariably left with five minutes in which to do it! Over the years I have perfected a quick five-minute routine which works for the majority of women using the minimum of colours and tools. I will take you through this routine step by step, with easy-to-follow instructions and diagrams. At first it may take you longer than five minutes, but with a little practice you'll soon be able to achieve perfect results in those rushed few minutes you have on busy mornings. Take note of the following tips.

An easy make-up routine can be perfected in five minutes.

MOISTURISE BEFORE APPLYING MAKE-UP

It is important to moisturise your skin before applying any cosmetics to allow them to glide on evenly and not stick in heavier patches to dry or flaky areas of skin. Moisturise your whole face, including lips, eyes and neck – be careful not to get moisturiser on eyelashes as this can cause mascara to slide off during the day. It is best to let moisturiser sink into the skin before applying make-up (for at least ten minutes), so I would advise you to apply it as soon as you rise and wash and leave it on over breakfast. Never forget your neck: the skin on your neck ages 15 years before your face – you may look 40 but your neck may look 55!

cosmetic
sponge

powder brush

eye-shadow spoolie

lip brush

blusher brush

eye-shadow blending brush

TOOLS

FOR A
FLAWLESS
FINISH

ALWAYS APPLY MAKE-UP IN GOOD LIGHT

Make sure the mirror you use for applying make-up is in good, natural daylight. The best solution is to place it on a bedroom or bathroom window-ledge so that the daylight is shining directly on to your face. If this is not possible, and you need to apply make-up by electric light, make sure you have lights on each side of the mirror so that one side of your face is not in shadow. Bulbs completely surrounding a mirror are ideal – and make you feel like a film star!

THE TOOLS YOU NEED

- Cosmetic sponge (optional)
- Large powder brush or puff
- Double-ended sponge eye-shadow applicator spoolie
- Lip brush (optional)
- Blusher brush
- Eye-shadow blending brush (optional)

STEP-BY-STEP FIVE-MINUTE GUIDE

STEP 1 BASE PRODUCTS

Your complexion will always benefit from using a base – not only because it will look smoother and flawless but it will be protected from the weather and central heating. If you do not like the feel of foundation – although many today, being water based, are *very* light – try a tinted moisturiser or even mix a small amount of fake tan into your moisturiser each morning.

Always select a base colour which is as close to your *natural* colour as possible. Buy it in natural daylight – take it to the shop door/window with a hand mirror and test it on your jawline, *not* your hand.

TO APPLY

Dot the foundation all over your face – forehead, cheeks, nose, chin, eyes and lips – keeping mostly to the centre and away from your hair. With your fingers (or a damp cosmetic sponge if you keep it scrupulously clean), sweep the foundation outwards towards the sides of your face, making sure it is well blended at the jaw and hairline. If the colour is a good match to your skin tone (never lighter or darker), you will not need to continue blending down your neck! *(This takes approximately 1 minute.)*

STEP 2   CONCEALER   *(if necessary)*

Some dark circles under the eye are not caused by poor diet or lack of sleep, but by very thin skin under the eyes which shows the bluey haemoglobin colour of the blood beneath. If this is a permanent feature, it is worth investing in a concealer stick (one shade lighter than your foundation) to cover these areas quickly after applying the foundation. *(This takes approximately 30 seconds.)*

'I have a drawer full of the stuff, but only use a few bits and pieces.'

Patricia, age 23

STEP 3   POWDER   *(if necessary)*

Not every woman likes to use powder as it can give a heavy, matt look and settle in lines and wrinkles making them more prominent. If this is the case, try a very light *translucent* powder and keep it to the nose, cheeks and chin and away from any lines on the forehead or around the mouth and eyes. The majority of women, however, will benefit from a quick whisking of powder with a large brush over the entire face – particularly eyes, cheeks and lips which will help eye-shadow, blusher and lipstick stay on longer. *(This takes about 30 seconds.)*

STEP 4   EYES

Firstly, pencil in those all-important eyebrows which should have been plucked and thinned into an elegant shape. Then outline the outside corners of the eye only with a soft pencil. Now coat the entire eye area with a pale, highlight shadow (the whole eyelid right up to the eyebrow) with a sponge applicator. With a darker eye-shadow make a 'wish-bone' shape on the outside edge of the eye with the other end of the sponge applicator. Blend the darker eye-shadow colour into the lighter one with finger or small blending brush. Now finish off with mascara, completing bottom lashes first and then the top ones. *(This takes approximately 1½ minutes.)*

VARIATIONS FOR DIFFERENT EYES

If your eyes are *droopy*, at the sides, take the 'wishbone' shape as high as possible towards your eyebrow (see far right picture).

If your eyes are *close-set*, keep the eyelid area near the nose as light as possible and emphasise the eye-pencil at the outer eye.

If your eyes are *wide-set*, take the top part of the 'wishbone' shape as far as possible towards the nose, and continue the eye-pencil towards the nose also.

If your eyes are *very large*, put the eye pencil on the *inside* of your lashes.

If your eyes are *very small*, use a white pencil inside the eyelashes and elongate the eyes with the darker pencil as much as possible.

If your eyes are *deep-set/sunken*, use only the paler shadow without the 'wishbone' effect. Use pencils to emphasise eyes and brows.

If your eyes are *prominent*, emphasise the 'wishbone' effect as much as possible to create a crease in the eyelid.

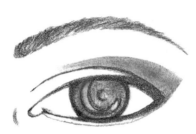

Outline the outer edge of the eye with eye pencil. Cover the entire eye in a light shadow and use a darker shadow for the 'wishbone' shape.

STEP 5 BLUSHER

This is the step you can always drop out if you are in a real rush (eye-pencils and lipsticks have most effect). Once you know *exactly* where to put it, however, blusher can be quick and easy to apply.

WHERE TO START

Smile at yourself in the mirror and put the first dab of a light powder blusher on the 'apple' of the cheek directly under the eyeball. From here, sweep light strokes of blusher up towards the top of the ear keeping the colour on the top of the cheekbone, *not* beneath it. If you have not used any powder on the face, a cream or gel blusher can be applied in exactly the same place using the fingertips instead of a brush. *(This takes approximately 30 seconds.)*

BLUSHER AND LIPSTICK

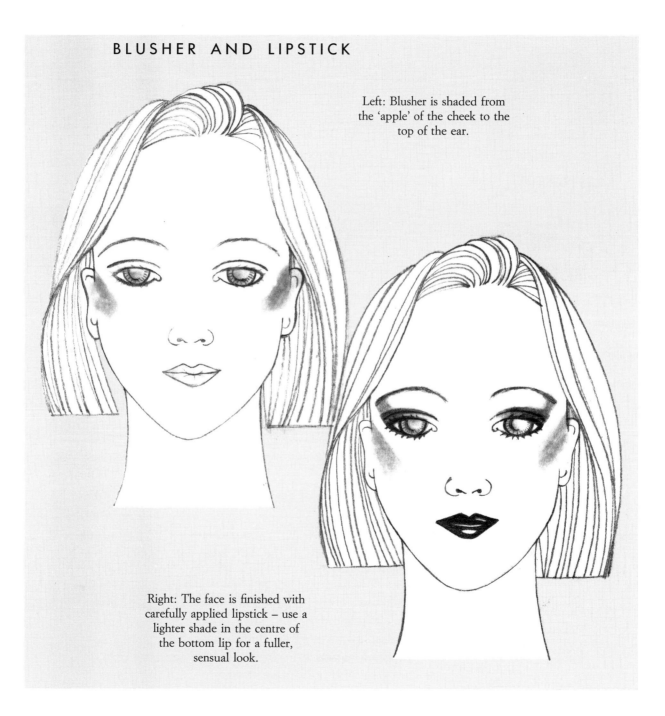

Left: Blusher is shaded from the 'apple' of the cheek to the top of the ear.

Right: The face is finished with carefully applied lipstick – use a lighter shade in the centre of the bottom lip for a fuller, sensual look.

Above: For a more glamorous evening look, strengthen your eye make-up and blusher and add a brighter shade of lipstick.

Opposite: Holiday make-up needs to look and feel natural – keep it simple with tinted moisturiser, creamy blusher and lip gloss.

STEP 6 LIPS

(a) Firstly, outline the lips with a lip pencil – this is particularly important to stop 'feathering' of lipstick and to give a good outline to your lips if they are 'blurred' at the edges. Use a pencil just slightly darker than your lipstick shade but not so dark as to be noticeable.

(b) Create a nice 'Cupid's bow' if yours is not too strong, but don't take the pencil right into the corners of the mouth as it can easily look smudged there.

(c) To make the upper and lower lips less full, draw the line just inside the natural lip-line – make sure lips have been covered in foundation and powder before you do this or the natural lip colour will show.

(d) To make the upper or lower lip fuller, draw the line slightly outside the natural lip-line – you need a steady hand to do this or it can look messy!

(e) Colour inside the lip-pencil line with your selected shade of lipstick using a lip brush, lip wand (sponge) or the lipstick bullet itself if you are careful.

(f) If one lip is fuller than the other, use a darker shade of lipstick on the fuller lip and a lighter one on the thinner lip. This helps balance them out. (*This takes approximately 1 minute.*)

EVENING TIPS

The make-up routine previously outlined is a restrained, fairly natural daytime look. For the evening, when lighting is artificial and harsher, you may want to heighten your make-up for a more glamorous look. Make the following amendments for a quick transformation:

- Moisten a cotton ball/pad with mild toner and wipe forehead, nose and chin area.
- Remove lipstick with a tissue.
- Reapply foundation to forehead, nose, lips and chin.
- Dust face with translucent powder.

- Add a little frosted shadow to centre of eyelid and orbital bone – gold or silver can look fun for a party.
- Deepen the 'wishbone' effect with a stronger colour.
- Add a deeper shade of blusher beneath the cheekbones to accent hollows.
- Reapply lipstick in a stronger shade.
- Put a dab of lip gloss (or a lighter lipstick shade) on the centre of the bottom lip for a sensual look.
- Add another coat of mascara and strengthen the effect of eye and eyebrow pencils.
- If your eyelashes are sparse, chop up some false eyelashes and apply lashes individually with tweezers – if you have the patience!
- If you like liquid eyeliner, it can look great for evenings – remember to lean your hand on your cheekbone for a non-wobbly line!

'I'd like to experiment a bit more – I've done it this way for years.'

Dawn, age 38

HOLIDAY MAKE-UP

No one wants to be coated in heavy, matt make-up on a hot, sunny holiday. A golden, healthy translucent look is attractive and easy to achieve with the following holiday make-up kit:

- tinted moisturiser
- fake-tan (to mix with moisturiser nightly)
- bronzing powder or gel
- cream or gel blusher
- waterproof mascara and remover
- eye-pencils (forget the shadows)
- sheer lipstick
- lip gloss or gel
- pale nail polish (looks great with a tan)
- nail polish remover (I always forget it!)

MAKE-UP WITH GLASSES

SHORT SIGHTED

If you are short sighted, your eyes will look smaller behind your concave lenses. You should therefore aim to make your eyes look bigger both with eye-pencils and by sweeping the 'wishbone' shape out and as high as possible. Keep the inside of the eyelid as light as possible and a dab of highlighter in the centre will help enlarge the eyes. Plenty of mascara will help enormously.

LONG SIGHTED

Always use a magnifying mirror to apply your make-up, or the special magnifying make-up glasses with 'tip-down' lenses to make-up one eye at a time. Your convex lenses will magnify your eyes, so it is best to keep eye make-up as simple and discreet as possible. Steer clear of bright eye-shadows and pencils and fibrous mascaras which can leave 'blobs' on the lashes. Dark circles under your eyes and wrinkles around them will be magnified, so keep the concealer but do away with powder.

'STAYING PUT' UNDER GLASS

Glasses trap the heat next to your face making creamy eye-shadows, pencils, mascaras and even blushers smudge and shift position. Always use matt, powder shadows and blushers and invest in an eye-shadow base or fix to apply before the shadow to keep it in place. If you have long lashes which leave smudges of mascara on your lenses, seal them with a coat of colourless mascara.

ADJUSTING BLUSHER FOR GLASSES

If your glasses have very broad or very high 'arms', you may need to adjust the position of your blusher slightly. If the arms of the glasses are sitting directly on and covering your cheekbone completely, position your blusher just a little lower to create a hollow beneath your cheekbone. Still curve inwards towards your nose – never create a straight line downwards towards your mouth as this gives a very false, gaunt look.

Always balance the shade of your glasses frame with a similar strength lipstick so one does not overpower the other.

SELECTING
COSMETIC COLOURS

In the last chapter I described how you have a choice between harmonious or conflicting clothing colours, depending on the impact you wish to make, the confidence you have in your looks, and your personality type. Similarly with cosmetics, you can opt for a harmonious look with shades similar to your own Colour Direction, or you can create an impact with an opposing direction to your own. Listed below are the harmonious colours for each Colour Direction – but feel free to break the rules if fashion or your personality dictates otherwise.

DEEP DIRECTION

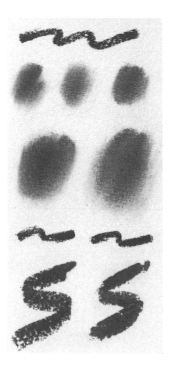

Brows	■ dark brown or black pencil to blend with your natural colour
Eyes	■ choose colours which complement (not match) your eye colour
Eyeliner	■ black, charcoal or brown for day
	■ navy or teal for an evening change
Eye-shadow	■ highlight – icy beige (silver for evening)
	■ wishbone – grey or navy
	■ evening colours – deep purple or green
Mascara	■ black or brown/black
	■ purple or navy for evening
Blush	■ deep berry, burgundy or browny red
Lips	■ select shades to match your outfit
Pencil	■ red or rust (depending on lipstick colour)
Lipstick	■ red, deep pinks, terracotta
Lipgloss	■ clear red

LIGHT DIRECTION

Brows	■ beige or taupe to blend with natural colour
Eyes	■ choose colours which complement (not match) natural colour
Eyeliner	■ soft brown or grey for day
	■ soft navy can be good for evening
Eye-shadow	■ highlight – pink or peach (gold for evening)
	■ wishbone – soft brown or grey
	■ evening colours – soft green or navy
Mascara	■ brown or black/brown
	■ soft navy or teal for evening
Blush	■ soft pinks, coral and peach
Lips	■ select shades to match your outfit
Pencil	■ coral will suit most lipsticks
Lipstick	■ pinks, coral, peach, raspberry red
Lipgloss	■ translucent peach

BRIGHT DIRECTION

Brows	■ brown or grey to blend with natural colour
Eyes	■ choose colours which complement (not match) your eye colour
Eyeliner	■ grey or black for day
	■ navy or teal for evening
Eye-shadow	■ highlight – icy beige (silver for evening)
	■ wishbone – navy, charcoal
	■ evening colours – soft purple, deep turquoise
Mascara	■ black or brown/black
	■ purple or teal for evening
Blush	■ clear pink or peach
Lips	■ select shades to match your outfit
Pencil	■ red or coral to suit lipstick
Lipstick	■ bright red, coral (or even fuchsia!)
Lipgloss	■ clear red

MUTED DIRECTION

Brows	■ beige, taupe or grey to match your natural colour
Eyes	■ choose colours which complement (not match) your eye colour
Eyeliner	■ taupe or brown for day ■ moss green or teal for evening
Eye-shadow	■ highlight – beige or peach (gold for evening ■ wishbone – mink or grey ■ evening colours – sage green or plum
Mascara	■ brown or black/brown ■ teal or plum for evenings
Blush	■ peach, salmon or brown
Lips	■ select shades to match your outfit
Pencil	■ coral or dusty pink to match lipstick
Lipstick	■ toffee, rose pink, soft red
Lipgloss	■ clear pink or russet

WARM DIRECTION

Brows	■ chestnut or auburn to match natural colour
Eyes	■ choose colours which complement (not match) your eye colour
Eyeliner	■ brown or taupe for day ■ green or amethyst for evening
Eye-shadow	■ highlight – beige or peach (gold for evening) ■ wishbone – brown or teal for day ■ evening colours – copper, green or turquoise
Mascara	■ brown for day ■ teal for evening
Blush	■ apricot, peach or nutmeg
Lips	■ select shades to match your outfit
Pencil	■ deep coral will suit all lipsticks
Lipstick	■ terracotta, salmon, coral, warm red
Lipgloss	■ clear russet

COOL DIRECTION

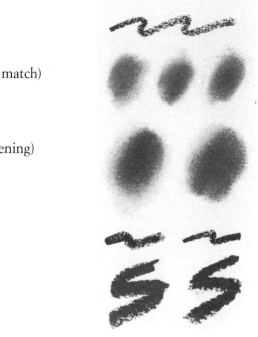

Brows	■ grey or beige to match natural colour
Eyes	■ choose colours which complement (not match) eye colour
Eyeliner	■ grey or black for day
	■ navy or blue for evening
Eye-shadow	■ highlight – icy beige, pink (silver for evening)
	■ wishbone – navy or charcoal for day
	■ purple or plum for evening
Mascara	■ black for day
	■ navy or plum for evening
Blush	■ rose pinks
Lips	■ select shades to match your outfit
Pencil	■ raspberry works well with all lipsticks
Lipstick	■ rose, fuchsia, red
Lipgloss	■ clear wine coloured

CHAPTER EIGHT

INTERPRETING THE CATWALK

*E*VERYONE CAN FOLLOW fashion, enjoy fashion and keep adapting to the latest trends well into old age. Many women, however, equate 'fashion' only with what they see on the catwalks and the glossy pages of the magazines and supplements. As these images are often 'over the top' and outrageous, 'fashion' is often dismissed as crazy, out-of-touch and unwearable by the ordinary woman in the street. As a consequence, many women become stuck in a fashion rut, fright-

ened to change or experiment with new ideas for fear of looking ridiculous. The result is that such women can then start to look dowdy, old fashioned and often older than they could look.

It is important to remember that catwalk fashion is not meant to represent what you should wear on the street – the fact that Edina in *Absolutely Fabulous* copies the catwalk exactly is what makes her character so entertaining to look at! The designers are in a fiercely competitive business in which publicity is everything. Getting their name and pictures splashed across the international press is the main aim of catwalk shows to sell not only clothes but, most importantly, the perfumes, cosmetics and accessories associated with the name.

The press, of course, fall for it every time, printing the most eye-catching pictures they can get their hands on: 10" (25cm) platform shoes, safety-pinned clothing; bare bosoms, stomachs and bottoms; and the most outrageous headgear, from a nun's wimple to a bird's nest-hat, complete with eggs! Fashion shows are also theatre –

'Fashion can be anything from a classic suit to a mini-skirt and Doc Martens.'

Marie, age 24

style

circus even – very entertaining and great fun to attend.

Amongst all the creative gimmickry, however, are the signals of the true trends of the season. You need to be able to 'read' catwalk pictures and look for the themes and trends that run consistently through all the collections. It is these signals that the buyers and designers for the high-street stores will pick up on to create the 'wearable' outfits for you and I.

As I mentioned earlier in Chapter 3, designers are simply influenced by everything that is happening socially, economically and politically around them. All they do is exaggerate those influences in their designs. The Nineties have seen huge interest and concern for the environment and ecological issues, which has manifested itself in many 'tribal' looks on the catwalk. If you see a model in a magazine with twigs in her hair, mud on her face, a bone through her nose and a sack for a dress, you are not meant to take it literally! The message is that fashion has returned to all things natural: unstructured hair, natural make-up, ethnic jewellery, earthy colours and non-synthetic fabrics.

These catwalk messages become easy to spot when you train your eye. Look for the predominant colours within a season; the shape of jackets; the length of skirts; the width of belts; the type of accessories; the favoured fabrics and patterns; and which part of the body is the current focal point – bust, waist, hips, legs, etc.

The glossy magazine pictures will also point you in the right direction of the current hair and make-up styles. Once you are aware of what the current trends, themes, colours and accessories are, you can decide to what degree you want to incorporate them into your wardrobe.

YOUR FASHION PERSONALITY

How much of the new looks you decide to adopt depends on your 'fashion personality'. Some style consultants like to analyse your personality as 'romantic', 'dramatic', 'natural', etc, but I always find these labels totally inadequate as women can be a mixture of all these traits – emphasising one over the others on different occasions. For a walk in the country, I like to look 'natural'; for a party I go a little more 'dramatic'; my nightwear is definitely 'romantic' – but for some reason they *never* have a 'slob' category, which is how I often look when relaxing at home!

Rather than putting your personality into a pigeon-hole, I think it is easier to think about your 'fashion personality' which is usually far more consistent and easily covers all your moods – romantic, dramatic, natural, slobby or otherwise. Like your body shape and colouring, your fashion personality can change throughout your life, from being a trendsetter in your teens/twenties; to contemporary in your thirties/forties; to classic in your fifties and beyond. Some women's fashion taste never changes: they remain a trendsetter from their teens to their dying day; and some may even be quite classic in their youth and metamorphose into a trendsetter (often after divorce!) in later life.

It is your fashion personality that gives you your individual look. The advice I have given in the preceding chapters on hair, clothing, colour and accessories can be interpreted very differently by two very different personalities. Two women could both have angular faces, curved body outlines, similar figure concerns and deep colouring. My advice: keep angles around the face; waist emphasis in the body; deep, strong colours next to the face, etc. The first woman, who is a trendsetter, might interpret this with a spiky hairstyle, zig-zag earrings, a slash-neck, fuchsia, belted sweater, and tight black trousers with ankle boots. The second woman, who is more classic, may opt for a neat 'bob' hairstyle, a navy fitted blazer and tapered skirt, square gold earrings and court shoes. My advice is the same – the missing ingredient is *your* fashion personality.

TRENDSETTER

For a trendsetting look, team up a blazer with a knotted denim shirt, T-shirt, jeans and deck shoes.

CLASSIC

The classic blazer look with
pleated skirt, tailored blouse, silk
scarf and loafers.

CONTEMPORARY

A beret, lambswool sweater and
skirt give the blazer a
contemporary twist.

TRENDSETTER

The trendsetter is often, but not always, young – perhaps we should say 'young at heart'. She likes to be noticed and is often outgoing and an extrovert personality. If she is older, she may be working in a particularly creative field – especially fashion itself – where it is accepted, if not expected, to have a trendsetting look. She will follow and apply catwalk looks very closely and is not afraid to incorporate most of the new ideas into her wardrobe. She probably really loves clothes and has a high turnover of them. They do not need to be expensive (although they can be very expensive designer items); what is more important is that they are the latest trend or fad. The trendsetter will often have exaggerated hairstyles and make-up and will not be afraid to try unusual colour combinations and mixtures of patterns. Her accessories may be oversized and dramatic – always obvious.

CONTEMPORARY

Most women in their twenties and thirties class themselves as contemporary; many women over thirty want to look contemporary but don't know how to, and therefore stick to a classic look. The contemporary woman knows how to read a trendsetting, catwalk look and adapt it into her wardrobe. Seeing a picture of a model with a huge flowery hat; a string-vest top; a pendant (like a door knocker on a rope); bell-bottom trousers and 4″ (10cm) platform shoes, she will purchase a small hat with one flower; a crochet sweater; a small pendant on a thong; slightly wider trousers than normal; and ½″ (1cm) platform shoes. She is always interested in clothes and accessories and likes to buy new pieces each season, but also keeps a core of more timeless pieces to which she adds the fashionable items. Her hair and make-up will change over the years but probably not from season to season.

CLASSIC

The classic fashion personality is more restrained and may not be interested in the latest trends and fads. She prefers to stick to the same styles and colours and is often interested in value-for-money in

her clothing as she expects to keep garments for a long time and obtain good wear from them. She has probably also worn the same hairstyle and make-up for many years and selects jewellery and accessories for their quality rather than noticeability. Some younger women have a naturally classic fashion personality which they retain forever, other women may find that they travel towards a classic look as they get older. If you feel you are stuck in a classic rut and would like to look more contemporary, begin by introducing current accessories to your wardrobe; then small garments (such as waistcoats); and maybe then update your hairstyle and buy a new lipstick or eye-shadow. It is amazing how a few changes on the outside can make you feel younger and livelier on the inside!

ADAPTATIONS TO AGE

This is a tricky topic! I would never dictate to women that, once they reach a certain age, they should stop wearing bright colours, short skirts, body-conscious clothes, etc. This really does depend on an individual's personality, colouring and the shape their particular body is in. One only has to look at Joan Collins, Tina Turner and Sophia Loren to realise that age is but a number, and these days you can keep yourself looking as young as you feel.

However, you may not have the time or money for personal exercise trainers, hairdressers, masseurs, dressers or cosmetic artists to be at your constant beck and call, so I will give the following advice to those who have, perhaps, succumbed a little to the advancing years:

- **If you have a double chin**, avoid high necklines, chokers and scarves worn inside blouse/shirt collars. Keep to lower, open necklines to create the illusion of a longer, slimmer neck. Necks which are wrinkled, but have remained undropped, are better with higher necklines, scarves, etc.
- **Slack, flabby upper arms** are always ageing. Wear elbow-length

A crazy, ethnic catwalk look can find itself diluted to an indo-chine suit on the high street.

or three-quarter length sleeves in summer and invest in shawls and wraps for strappy evening or summer wear.

- **Long hair worn down** often gives the impression of an older woman trying to recapture her youth. Best to wear it up in an elegant style or have a short, chic cut.

- **Don't let your bosom succumb to gravity** – remember to be measured regularly for new bras – 90 percent of older women wear the wrong size! A large, low bust can look very matronly and needs a 'straight' style of clothing if it makes you very short waisted.

- **Hair dyed back to its original colour** will make skin and eyes look dull and faded. As hair goes grey, skin and eyes also lose pigment – you therefore cannot go back to your original hair colour without an ageing effect on your complexion and eyes. Best to colour your hair a mid-brown or even lighter.

- **Yellow-grey or salt 'n' pepper hair** can look dowdy and often gives a 'jaundiced' look to the skin, unlike silver grey or white hair which can look sharp and dynamic. A woman who was originally a natural redhead will always grey to a salt 'n' pepper colour and is best to colour her hair a warm brown or honey blonde.

- **Tight perms age the most!** A softer or straighter hairstyle is often more flattering on an older woman. Break out of a rut and ask your hairdresser to show you new styling methods and products such as mousse, setting sprays and gels.

Tight perms, tight clothes and tiny accessories age the most . . .

- **Facial lines will become more apparent** if heavily powdered. If you have lines around the eyes and forehead, leave the powder off these areas and just dab your cheeks, nose and chin. Similarly, shiny or frosted eye-shadow will accentuate slack or 'crepey' eyelids – stick to matt shadows or forget shadow altogether and use lots of eye-pencil and mascara.

- **Tiny jewellery and other accessories**, particularly if you are fuller figured or large boned, can give the 'little old lady' look; conversely too much jewellery can give the 'mutton-dressed-as-lamb' look. A happy medium is to make a statement with one

eye-catching item – a good leather belt, a gold pendant, some stylish earrings – for a mature but fashionable look.

- **Keep up with fashion trends** – nothing will make you look older than outdated clothes. If you are still wearing polyester 'pussy cat bow' blouses, crimplene trousers and a Pac-a-mac, throw caution to the wind and send the whole lot to Oxfam. Treat yourself to a cotton-knit sweater, some roomy linen trousers and a gorgeous swing raincoat. Add some large wooden beads or pendant, some soft suede loafers, and watch the years fade away . . .

Don't be afraid to keep up with fashion trends if your body and personality can carry them off well.

THE SEVEN DEADLY SINS OF STYLE

Although I have advocated fashion freedom very strongly throughout this book, there are half a dozen fashion gaffes which, although seen often for publicity purposes on catwalks, can look disastrous on mere mortals. These are my seven all-time favourites:

1 **Feet first.** Shoes are number one on my list because, they can really make or break an outfit. On colour, the general rule is that shoes should be the same intensity or darker than the hemline and *never* lighter. Taking that to its logical conclusion, the only time white shoes should be worn is with a white skirt/trousers or with a dress/skirt where white is predominant in the pattern. White shoes and dark skirts never!

2 **Tight situation.** The right shoe, however, is nothing without the correct leg coverage, particularly with ankle boots. Stock up on opaque tights in dark shades or ribbed woollen tights to complement the lace-up 'granny' boots. For an attractive, fashionable look, the skirt, hemline and boot should all blend together – particularly if the skirt is split. The smartest look of all is brown skirt, melting into brown ribbed tights, blending into brown laced boots. The worst look of all is black slit skirt, contrasted with suntan tights, finished off with black patent stilettos!

3 **The bottom line.** I will be brief (excuse the pun) on this one, as we all know the horrors of the dreaded VPL (visible panty line). When wearing tight-fitting leggings, ski-pants and jodhpurs, do make sure that there are no unsightly bulges from bikini-style briefs. Thong-style briefs are ideal for those with slim bottoms; while the broader-of-beam need waist-high control briefs. Skirts should *never* be tight enough to show a VPL. Can you turn your skirt easily around your body and insert two fingers comfortably in the waistband?

4 **Jacket potato.** On the subject of jackets, never wear a double-breasted jacket open as this has the result of turning you into a shapeless sack of potatoes. Double-breasted jackets are made to be worn closed (except when seated, of course) and as a consequence lose their shape (and yours) completely when left dangling in mid-air. Pass this advice on to your man too!

5 **Cliff hangers.** Large bosoms (a problem for some and the envy of many) need to beware two potential pitfalls: long scarves and necklaces which can look very silly dangling precariously over the precipice; and breast-pockets – particularly those with bright, shiny buttons strategically placed! Enough said.

6 **Headline news.** The 'hat-worn-as-halo' is my all-time favourite and simply cannot be excluded from my list of ghastly fashion gaffes. Weddings always remind me of school nativity plays. Remember: keep it down to the eyebrows – you can't see much, but how others see you scores 101 percent in the sartorial stakes.

7 **Balancing act.** Bulging shoulder-bags performing a balancing act on ample hips/bottoms are not a pretty sight – particularly when they are also in an eye-catching colour and made of a shiny leather or plastic. As the eye is always drawn to light and/or shiny objects, choose darker, matt handbags or clutch bags or make sure a shoulder bag has a length of strap which does not position it right on your widest point.

Can you spot the 7 Deadly Style Sins?

FASHION MYTHS

There are some fashion sayings that have been uttered so many times that we accept them without question. However, times have changed and some of those myths can now be exploded:

1 ***Natural fibres are always best.*** Not any more. Synthetic fabrics have changed dramatically since the days of crimplene skirts and nylon blouses! Technological advances mean new fabrics 'breathe' like their natural counterparts and can have all the desired aesthetic and tactile properties while being cheaper, colour-fast and machine washable. Many top designers are now using synthetic fibres in their collections – 100 percent polyester is not the frowned-upon label it used to be as technical developments have vastly improved its qualities. The introduction of Lycra has led to a whole new category of figure-skimming clothes which would never have been made before. And two of the latest innovations, Tactel and Supplex, are both nylon fibres, but with the feel and comfort of cotton.

2 ***Less is more.*** This is often true, but not always! A very plain, unadorned outfit worn with natural hair and make-up can simply look dull – unless you look like a supermodel. Most of us need a superb hairstyle, immaculate make-up and maybe one stunning accessory to carry off a totally plain style without looking, well, plain. However, don't be caught trying too hard.

3 ***Shoes and bag should always match.*** This is an old-fashioned idea which can now be ignored. Of course you can match if you want to but today you can choose anything that looks good with what you're wearing. If you're wearing black and brown, a brown bag with black shoes can look great. Usually you'll look better if your shoes are darker than your bag because you'll look more balanced.

4 ***Everything comes back into fashion.*** It's true that fashion is constantly being recycled with only a few totally new ideas every now and then. So if you have the space to keep your past purchases,

'Less is more' – don't be caught trying too hard.

then do. You will find, though, that when a particular look comes round again it will be in a slightly different form from it's original incarnation – so be prepared to have things altered slightly or to wear them in a different way. Don't forget also that you are now older and possibly a different shape – so what suited you then may not suit you now.

5 **Coats should be longer than skirts.** Not any more. Short swing coats over long skirts and finger-tip length coats are very chic with only a fraction of a short skirt peeping below. The only real disaster is a very long coat with an even longer skirt drooping below it.

6 **Jewellery metals shouldn't be mixed.** Yes they can – and they can look sensational if you do it well. A mixture of gold and silver bangles, or a stack of different rings, looks modern and fun. It has to look deliberate, however, and not accidental – a silver chain worn with gold earrings looks odd, but silver and gold chains mixed together with either gold or silver earrings works well.

'I'm scared of being mutton-dressed-as-lamb.'

Maureen, age 48

CHAPTER NINE

*'I want to look modern –
but not a fashion victim.'*

Margaret, age 39

Your

I N THIS CHAPTER, I will put all the theory from the previous chapters into practice by taking you 'behind the scenes' on some of the makeovers I have performed for television, magazines and newspapers. From an initial 'before' photograph, I analyse facial features, figure outline, proportions and colouring and then make my decisions for best hairstyle, accessories, clothes and cosmetics accordingly – always, of course, taking into account the individual woman's fashion personality, lifestyle and wardrobe needs.

At the end of any makeover I always present my brave volunteer with her own 'Personal Profile' booklet containing all the information used to complete her transformation. This way she will be able to look and feel good, not just for one day, but *every* day in the future – even as fashion colours and styles come and go. If you would like your own Personal Profile to discover your hidden potential, see page 160 for details of how to apply.

potential

MAKEOVER 1

For WeightWatchers' *Slim and Trim* magazine

PERSONAL DETAILS

Name: Erica
Age: Late 30's
Needs: To find which styles suit her 'new' body after losing over five stone at WeightWatchers.

FACE AND FIGURE ANALYSIS

Face: ROUND OUTLINE. Erica's hair is too flat on top for a round face – it needs more height on top to elongate it, keeping little width at the sides.

Features: Her almond eyes, straight nose and cheekbones will be best complemented by angular earrings and necklines.

Figure: STRAIGHT OUTLINE (wide ribcage with little waist-emphasis).

Proportions: Short neck, large bust, and wide hips/thighs.

STYLE RECOMMENDATIONS

Erica needs to keep a straight silhouette to her clothing with no horizontal line around her wide waist area. She is best advised to steer clear of belts or tucked-in in tops and opt instead for long blouses, tunics, waistcoats and jackets – making sure they end below the widest part of her hips/thighs. Straight skirts and trousers will complement these tops. Erica also needs a lower neckline to elongate her neck and should keep her bust and hip area plain and free from pockets and other details.

Colouring: Blonde hair, blue eyes, light (freckled) complexion.

Colour Direction: Erica's Colour Direction is LIGHT which is complemented by the light cosmetic shades (taupe eyeshadow, coral blush and lipstick), ivory waistcoat and pearl/diamanté earrings. The black trouser suit works well because of the lighter top and jewellery.

Fashion personality: Because of her previous weight, Erica had found it difficult to follow fashion but was pleased to discover she could now create a fashionable, CONTEMPORARY look with a capsule of separates to take her from day to evening.

YOUR POTENTIAL

PERSONAL DETAILS

Name: Sarla
Age: Twenties
Needs: To find her most flattering clothes and cosmetic shades, and an easy make-up routine – particularly for evenings after work.

MAKEOVER 2

For *Prima* magazine

FACE AND FIGURE ANALYSIS

Face: OVAL OUTLINE. Sarla has the perfect oval outline which takes most hairstyles well.
Features: Her curved features (arched eyebrows, soft nose, cheeks and lips) would be best suited, however, to a softer hairstyle rather than the angular bob currently worn. Contoured earrings and a soft, silky fabric next to the face will also work well.
Figure: CURVED OUTLINE (obvious waist emphasis).
Proportions: No particular problems! Sarla has the 'model' proportions of straight shoulders, small bust, long-waisted torso, and slim hips and thighs.

STYLE RECOMMENDATIONS

To make the most of her waistline, a wide belt in a contrasting colour was chosen to draw the eye. The horizontal stripes on the shoulder of the blouse also draw the eye to her wide shoulders and Sarla's flat hips and tummy are able to take a wide-pleated, above-the-knee skirt.
Colouring: Brown/black hair, dark brown eyes, deep complexion.
Colour Directions: Sarla's colouring is obviously DEEP but, although her skin is dark, it is a relatively 'light' tone of brown. The resulting contrast between her skin and hair (and skin and eyes) leads in the Secondary Direction of BRIGHT. Her best colours are DEEP BRIGHT ones (as shown in her 'after' picture) rather than the deep, muted shades of wine and navy worn in her 'before' picture. Shiny jewellery also complements her brightness.
Cosmetics: Charcoal eyeshadow and eyeliner with wine blush and lipstick.
Fashion personality: CONTEMPORARY. Sarla loved her new, vibrant look and easy to follow make-up routine.

MAKEOVER 3

For *Woman's Journal* Fashion Counsel

PERSONAL DETAILS

Name: Laura
Age: Teens
Needs: To achieve a small, flexible holiday wardrobe that is fun and fashionable.

FACE AND FIGURE ANALYSIS

Face: HEART-SHAPED OUTLINE. Laura's long straight hair is not the best style for her wide forehead and narrow chin. She needs to keep it close to her head at the top but with more fullness at the bottom.
Features: Her soft features will suit a curly hairstyle, rounded or scoop necklines and contoured, rather than angular jewellery shapes.
Figure: CURVED OUTLINE (obvious waist emphasis).
Proportions: Small bust, flat hips/thighs, slim calves.

STYLE RECOMMENDATIONS

Laura is able to wear body-hugging tops because of her small bust and narrow rib-cage. Also, her small bust allows her to wear long, chunky necklaces or pendants. Her slim hips enable her to tie a sarong directly at the hipline, and her slim legs make her one of the lucky women who can also wear a mid-calf skirt successfully.
Colouring: Red hair, hazel eyes and pale, freckled complexion.
Colour Direction: Laura's main Colour Direction is WARM which is complemented by earthy shades of rust, terracotta, mustard, etc. In her 'before' photo, she was wearing all cool colours (blue, white, red and black) without a warmer shade near the face to connect the clothing to her colouring.
Cosmetics: Peach and green eyeshadow, peach blusher and 'toffee' lipgloss. Translucent base to show freckles!
Fashion personality: TRENDSETTER – her mum had to fight to stop Laura wearing the 'Doc Marten' boots in the 'after' photo!

MAKEOVER 4

For *SHE magazine*

FACE AND FIGURE ANALYSIS

Face: RECTANGULAR OUTLINE. Pamela definitely suits a short hairstyle and would not suit any extra length with such a long face. Some degree of fringe is good to shorten the length of the face.

Features: Very angular and defined – straight eyebrows, eyes, nose and cheekbones with a strong jawline. Pamela's hair would benefit from a more angular cut, particularly a sharper cut around the ears to show off the cheekbones.

Figure: STRAIGHT OUTLINE (wide shoulders, broad ribcage, narrow hips).

Proportions: Long neck, small bust, long waisted, flat hips.

STYLE RECOMMENDATIONS

Pamela needs to keep to angular necklines to complement her new, sharper hairstyle, and because of her long neck she is able to button her shirts/blouses fully to the top without looking 'suffocated'. Her small bust allows her to take detail over the bust area such as the novelty buttons on the shirt and features such as breast pockets or double-breasted buttons on jackets. Her straighter body outline is best suited to straight jacket shapes, without waist emphasis.

Colouring: Pamela's hair was just beginning to show signs of grey (but only a small percentage) but most of her hair was still dark, coupled with dark eyes, her colouring is in the DEEP Direction.

Colour Directions: To colour the grey and give a younger look, Pamela's hair was given a chestnut vegetable dye which had the effect of bringing more warmth to the skin and eyes. To maintain her professional image, the two strongest business colours of black and white were chosen for her trouser suit and shirt.

Cosmetics: Less is more as you get older! Simply a tinted moisturiser, brown/black mascara and russet lipstick.

Fashion personality: CLASSIC – but now leaning towards CONTEMPORARY. Pamela had not worn make-up or a trouser-suit to work before and loved her contemporary image.

PERSONAL DETAILS

Name: Pamela

Age: Fifties

Needs: To update her style from classic to contemporary while still looking appropriate for a high-powered job.

MAKEOVER 5

For *Woman's Journal* Fashion Counsel

FACE AND FIGURE ANALYSIS

Face: SQUARE OUTLINE. Janet's curly hairstyle simply needed styling with mousse to give a little more height at the front and a sharper, wedge-look to the bottom edge.

Features: Her very angular bone structure in the face needs to be echoed by sharper necklines and jewellery. The scoop-neck of the blouse in her 'before' photo does not enhance her face.

Figure: CURVED (waist emphasis, tapered ribcage, flared hips).

Proportions: Broad shoulders, small bust, long waisted.

STYLE RECOMMENDATIONS

Janet has a good figure which can be shown off with tucked-in tops, fitted jackets, tapered trousers, eye-catching belts, etc. Her small bust allows her to draw attention to her top half with colour, bold patterns or details eg the contrasting silver buttons on the jacket.

Colouring: Dark brown hair, bright blue/green eyes, fair complexion.

Colour Directions: Janet has startlingly vivid colouring which, because of the contrast, is definitely in the BRIGHT Direction. Her favourite colours of brown, cream and beige are not really her best as they are in the opposite muted direction. If she wants to continue wearing her favourite shades, she would be better to combine them with a brighter shade near the face, – eg coral, green or brilliant white. Her most useful neutral shades for wardrobe planning are black, navy and charcoal grey which team up well with sharp, bright colours. The black ski-pants look sensational with the blue jacket which really brings Janet's face to life and makes her eyes sparkle.

Cosmetics: Grey eyeliner, black mascara, coral blush and lips.

Fashion personality: CLASSIC. Janet likes quite simple clothes without too much jewellery and make-up – when wearing a very bright colour, such as the blue jacket, this is often essential for a sophisticated look.

PERSONAL DETAILS

Name: Janet
Age: Thirties
Needs: To discover an easy-to-follow wardrobe plan (including best neutrals) because of little time for shopping.

MAKEOVER 6

For *SHE* magazine

FACE AND FIGURE ANALYSIS

Face: HEART-SHAPED OUTLINE. Julie's hair was swept horizontally across her forehead from a side parting which only emphasised her wide forehead. As she is also petite, her long hair style was swamping her small frame and fine bone structure.

Features: Her contoured nose, cheeks and mouth need a soft hairstyle but her full, curly style, although soft, was too overpowering. Julie's hair was cut into a short style with wispy side pieces and a feathered, non-geometric fringe.

Figure: STRAIGHT OUTLINE (wide ribcage, flat hips/thighs).

Proportions: Sloping shoulders, small/no bust, long waisted.

STYLE RECOMMENDATIONS

Julie is an extremely slim size 8 who would not be flattered by tight, body-conscious clothing. To give a little more volume to her body – particularly the upper-part – a loose, layered style was chosen, comprising an overshirt, cropped knitted waistcoat and soft palazzo pants. Shoulder pads were needed to give a boost to her sloping shoulders and curved earrings suited her soft face.

Colouring: Blue/green eyes, 'mousey' hair, fair complexion.

Colour Direction: Julie's Direction is predominantly LIGHT and was made even more so with the addition of a few highlights in the hair. In her 'before' photo, Julie had been wearing all deep colours (black and charcoal) and was pleased to see how the lighter gingham check enhanced her colouring even though the waistcoat was deep red. Julie is slim enough to wear white trousers which always add extra inches to bottoms/thighs.

Cosmetics: Tinted moisturiser, concealer under eyes, light pink lipstick and blush, taupe eyeshadow, brown mascara.

Fashion personality: CONTEMPORARY. Julie was thrilled with her new look which was relaxed and comfortable for her lifestyle, but also modern and fashionable – not the typical dowdy look that mums can easily fall into!

PERSONAL DETAILS

Name: Julie

Age: Twenties

Needs: To find a fashionable but casual look for a busy mum of three young children – including twins!

MAKEOVER 7

For BBC's *Good Morning* and *Woman's Journal* Fashion Counsel

PERSONAL DETAILS

Name: Jackie
Age: Thirties
Needs: A comfortable, flexible wardrobe for a lifestyle which includes computer working from home and looking after a baby son.

FACE AND FIGURE ANALYSIS

Face: RECTANGULAR OUTLINE which really needs a fringe to shorten its length.
Features: Jackie's features are mostly angular with very straight eyebrows, prominent cheekbones, almond eyes and a thin, straight mouth. Her long, straight hair shows off her bone-structure well but, as she always wears it tied-back, she might as well have a short, sharp cut!
Figure: CURVED OUTLINE (waist emphasis, rounded hips).
Proportions: Jackie thought she was 'pear-shaped' because of her big hips but, because of her wide shoulders, she actually has a very balanced figure which does not need shoulder pads as a 'pear-shape' would.

STYLE RECOMMENDATIONS

Jackie looked fantastic in the pin-stripe trouser suit with her waist emphasised with the fob chain. The V-neckline of the shirt complements her angular face. The tapered-leg trousers are ideal for curvy figures such as Jackie's.
Colouring: Dark brown hair, hazel eyes, olive complexion.
Colour Directions: Jackie's colouring falls in the DEEP Direction and will become even deeper when she tans in the summer. Pale colours next to her face are not her best, but deep ones – warm or cool – look fantastic.
Cosmetics: Smokey-green eye-shadow and pencils, black mascara, cinnamon blush and a rust lipstick to match the colours in her cardigan.
Fashion personality: CONTEMPORARY. Jackie felt that her new clothes and make-up gave her more energy to work at home whereas before she had not bothered about her appearance if no one could see her! Looking good for yourself is just as important (if not more so) than looking good just for others.

MAKEOVER 8

For *SHE* magazine

PERSONAL DETAILS

Name: Helen
Age: Forties
Needs: A classic look for special occasions with the versatility to 'recycle' the clothes for different events.

FACE AND FIGURE ANALYSIS

Face: ROUND OUTLINE. Helen's hair needs a little more volume at the top and less bulk at the sides of her face to give her a longer face and slimmer neck.

Features: Soft nose, cheeks, lips and jawline which need contoured jewellery shapes, soft lines and fabrics at the neck, and a fringe with bounce and movement.

Figure: STRAIGHT (broad shoulders, wide ribcage, no waist emphasis).

Proportions: Short neck, large bust, rounded stomach/hips, fuller figure.

STYLE RECOMMENDATIONS

As Helen has a very short neck, she needs to select lower necklines to give the illusion of a longer, slimmer neck. A tucked-in style at the waistline is not her best look as it puts a horizontal line around her middle – if she does do this, a loose jacket (which buttons) on top, will create a good straight line past her waistline. Straight trousers or a straight skirt complete her best style.

Colouring: Mid-brown hair, hazel eyes, medium complexion.

Colour Directions: Golden lights were added to Helen's hair which changed her direction from DEEP TO MUTED as her hair was then a shade lighter than her eyes. This colouring looks wonderful in shades of coffee and cream which were chosen for Helen's embroidered jacket, body and trousers. Brushed gold earrings and strings of muted silver and gold pearls were the finishing touches.

Cosmetics: Bronze eye-shadow, brown pencil and mascara, with cinnamon blush and lipstick. Bronzing powder for evening.

Fashion personality: CLASSIC. Helen loved this stylish evening look which is a change from traditional black and more 'grown up' than girlish dresses. The jacket, body and trousers can all be teamed with other pieces for many different occasions.

MAKEOVER 9

For *Woman's Journal* Fashion Counsel

FACE AND FIGURE ANALYSIS

Face: DIAMOND OUTLINE. Mary's hair simply needs sharpening-up, especially around the ears where she does not need any extra width because of her cheekbones and glasses.

Features: Straight eyebrows, almond eyes, prominent cheekbones, straight nose – all angular features, which means Mary needs less-round glasses and a more angular neckline to her blouse.

Figure: STRAIGHT (wide ribcage and waist, flat thighs).

Proportions: Sloping shoulders, large/low bust, short waisted, rounded tummy.

STYLE RECOMMENDATIONS

Because Mary is so short-waisted, she has made her body bottom-heavy by tucking in her blouse and wearing a mid-calf skirt in her 'before' photo. By wearing a straight top over her skirt and taking-up her hemline (to below the knee) she would put the proportions of her body into balance. In her 'after' photo, the angular neckline of the blouse and jacket are superb for her face and the straightness of the blouse and jacket make her wide waist and short midriff disappear – her large bust also looks reduced when it is not appearing directly on the waistline. Mary's glasses were changed for a smaller, more angular pair that put her eyes at the centre rather than the top of the lens. The fashionable earrings and tasselled pendant complete her new, modern look.

Colouring: Grey hair, blue/grey eyes, fair complexion.

Colour Directions: Mary's colouring is predominantly in the COOL Direction, although there was a little yellow in her hair which was removed with L'Oreal Osmose Grey Shampoo.

Cosmetics: Taupe eyebrow pencil, grey eye-shadow and pencil, soft pink lipstick and blush, black mascara.

Fashion personality: CLASSIC, but Mary now has ambitions to become a mature model! She felt and looked years younger in her fashionable 'pyjama suit' and modern jewellery

PERSONAL DETAILS

Name: Mary
Age: Sixties
Needs: To be transformed from 'an ageing farmer's wife' into a glamorous grandmother.

MAKEOVER 10

For WeightWatchers *Slim and Trim* magazine and national TV and press advertising

FACE AND FIGURE ANALYSIS

Face: OVAL OUTLINE. Sam is lucky in that most hairstyles will suit her. As she is growing it at the moment and didn't want a cut, her hair was styled to give a windswept look for her 'sexy' image!

Features: Soft features with round eyes, curved eyebrows, soft cheeks and mouth, which were complemented by round gold earrings and a heart-shaped pendant.

Figure: CURVED OUTLINE. Sam's new slimline figure revealed a tapered ribcage with a small waistline, gently rounded hips and thighs.

Proportions: Long neck, broad shoulders, small bust, long-waist.

STYLE RECOMMENDATIONS

Sam's new figure has model-girl proportions, especially the broad shoulders and long ribcage which are the most slimming assets a woman can have! Her long, slim neck allows her to wear a polo-neck well and the thin vertically striped pattern emphasises her slim body. The short leather miniskirt has no waistband, which makes Sam's ribcage even longer – although she could wear very wide belts and still not look short waisted. The A-line shape of the skirt is ideal for curved hips but shiny leather should only be worn on slim bottoms like Sam's. The miniskirt looks less revealing when worn with opaque tights and substantial, rather than spindly, shoes.

Colouring: Blonde hair, hazel eyes, medium complexion.

Colour Direction: With hair much lighter than her eyes, Sam's colouring is definitely in the MUTED Direction, making the soft grey of her polo-neck top an ideal shade for next to the face. Other good shades for her would be olive, aubergine or brown.

Cosmetics: Cream and brown eye-shadow, salmon blush, burgundy lipstick and brown mascara.

Fashion direction: TRENDSETTER. Sam was delighted with her new image which resulted in her being selected for national television/ press advertising for WeightWatchers – wearing one of her dream outfits, a little, black dress.

PERSONAL DETAILS

Name: Sam

Age: Twenties

Needs: To wear something sexy and clinging to celebrate losing three stone at WeightWatchers.

CHAPTER TEN

*I*IF YOU FEEL you have been in a style rut for the last few years, there is nothing like a change of image to give yourself a boost. It always amazes me after completing a makeover, to see how differently a woman behaves when she sees her new look in the mirror. For me it is extremely rewarding to see the new confidence that emerges in the way she walks, laughs and smiles for the camera. There is no better tonic in the world than knowing you look good.

I am often accused of asking people to look glum in the 'before' photo and also of dressing them in the wrong clothes to make them

Your total self

look better in the 'after' photo. This is categorically untrue! I don't know whether other 'makeover experts' employ this trick but I always ask my volunteers to come to the studio dressed in something they wear frequently, and wearing their normal hairstyle and make-up. I always ask them to smile for the camera, although that is sometimes difficult, as I'm sure you will know, when you are not feeling your best.

The fact is, that our appearance has a great effect on our confidence and on how others see us and relate to us. Ultimately it can affect the success of our relationships and career. Research shows that appearance counts for 55 percent of another person's opinion of us – over half of our total impact. Our behaviour (confidence, eye-contact, body language etc) counts for 38 percent – but remember that that figure is affected greatly by how we feel about our looks, making the initial 55 percent even more important! This leaves only 7 percent for our 'content' or what we have to say for ourselves. Intellectually, we all like to think that appearance doesn't matter but it is a fact of life that it does – and has done since time began.

This does not mean therefore that everyone has to look smart – what matters is that you *like* how you look and that your appearance suits your personality, lifestyle, age and physical features and makes you feel confident and self-assured. Clothes, hairstyles and accessories all give out messages about you. People who boast, 'I don't care what I look like', are saying something about themselves by their decision not to 'dress up'. Their appearance is just as important to them as someone who takes two hours each day to get ready for work! Appearance is non-verbal communication which speaks volumes about your values, occupation, lifestyle, politics, class – and even sexual preferences, if that is an important aspect of yourself to express.

The message of this book is that personal style should be an expression of your total self. So many women spend their whole lives trying to look like someone else – a friend, a film star or a picture in a magazine – but this is never successful because they are not *you*. Accept your whole self and turn it confidently into your unique style. If you have an angular face don't try to soften it with frills and flounces but accentuate it as your unique signature; if you have a fuller figure don't try to look smaller but dress stylishly large; don't dwell on your bad points but accentuate your plus points; and, please, don't be afraid to enjoy the different colours and fashions as you get older if that has been one of your passions in your youth.

Above all, don't feel guilty about taking an interest in or spending money on how you look. It depresses me that so many women put themselves at the bottom of the list where priorities are concerned. *Everyone* else will benefit from *you* feeling confident and good about yourself.

So next time it comes to a close choice between a new pedestal mat for the toilet or a new pair of earrings – don't give it a second thought!

PERSONAL ADVICE FROM THE AUTHOR

Carol Spenser will provide you with your very own *PERSONAL PROFILE COLLECTION* containing:

- *Fashion Portfolio* of current styles to suit your figure and colouring
- *Detailed analysis* of your face and figure
- *Solutions* to your figure problems
- *A flexible wardrobe* plan for your lifestyle
- *Hairstyle* ideas for your face
- *Colour suggestions* for clothes and make-up
- *A Swatch Wallet* for near-face colours
- *A quality lipstick* selected for you.

Questions on the Personal Profile answered by Carol Spenser

1. How do I Apply?

You fill in a detailed questionnaire on your physical characteristics and fashion/colour preferences. Plus you send two recent colour photographs of yourself. Your form and photos are analysed by Carol and her trained staff for your individual Personal Profile to be produced.

2. How does the cost compare?

A full colour and style consultation with an experienced reputable consultant ranges from £90 to £120 depending on where you live. Colour analysis alone can cost upwards of £50. The Personal Profile Collection is therefore around one third of the price of a total image consultation – plus you also receive the current Fashion Portfolio, a colour swatch wallet and lipstick!

2. Are there other benefits?

All your advice is there in black and white for you to read and re-read at your leisure. Within a personal consultation, I have found that most clients retain only a third of the information given. Plus you can re-order the Fashion Portfolio at the special price of £5.50 to update your wardrobe – image consultants worldwide pay up to £15 for this seasonal fashion guide.

For only £29.95 – a saving of over £5.00 on the RRP of £35.00
Now *you* can join the exclusive group of women who have benefited from Carol's personal advice through her regular TV appearances and magazine makeovers by sending for your own Personal Profile Collection direct from her office.

☐ I enclose cheque/postal order for £29.95 (payable to Public Persona Ltd)

☐ I wish to pay by Access/Visa/Mastercard no: _____

Expiry date _____ Signature _____

Address _____

_____

_____ Postcode _____

Don't delay, return the slip below to receive your application form. Or telephone the credit card hotline on 01223 812737 or fax 01223 812853.

Return your completed slip to: Public Persona Ltd, The Vineyards, 129 High Street, Bottisham, Cambridge CB5 9BA

For readers in the United States of America, Australia and Sweden contact the address above or telephone the above number to obtain details of suppliers of the Personal Profile in your country.